Venetian

Rosemary Gemmell

http://www.rosemarygemmell.com

First published in 2018 as a Kindle edition

Copyright © Rosemary Gemmell 2018

www.rosemarygemmell.com

All rights reserved. No part of this publication may be reproduced, stored, or transmitted in any form, or by any means electronic, mechanical or photocopying, recording or otherwise, without the prior permission of the copyright owner.

Venetian Interlude is a work of fiction. Names, characters, places and incidents are the product of the author's imagination or are used fictitiously. Any resemblance to actual events, locales, or persons, living or dead, is purely coincidental

Grateful thanks to V Gemmell for her excellent content editing, proof-reading and suggestions.

Chapter One

Livy collected her case from the carousel with rising excitement. Soon, she would be standing in St Mark's Square at last, right in the heart of Venice. It might only be for a few days before boarding her cruise ship, but she would make the most of every minute.

It wasn't quite the romantic trip she had once envisioned but better to be alone than with the wrong man. Thankfully, she had rediscovered her own mind in time to avoid a commitment last year, when the guy she'd been seeing started talking about going to 'find himself' in Tibet.

She no longer cared whether or not he ever found his way back, a measure of how blindly she'd allowed the relationship to continue because the old childhood friend had seemed like a safe option. No doubt the death of her beloved mum had partly numbed her ability to think objectively for a while. It was now time to decide what *she* wanted from the rest of her life, to visit some of the countries on her must-see list. She'd been overwhelmed to discover that her mother had left her a substantial sum of money in the hope Livy might travel at last. And Venice was right at the top of that list.

As she trundled her case through the airport doors, the delicious heat welcomed her. She'd decided to spare no expense and had booked a private water taxi to take her into Venice in style. A friend told her it was the best way to arrive the first time to a city built on a lagoon. Sure enough, the water taxi stand was only a few yards from the airport doors and her excitement mounted at every step.

Only one motor boat appeared to be waiting. The young dark-haired hunk who was obviously the driver stood in animated discussion with a tall man in light chinos and smart sea blue shirt who had his back to her, a sweater slung casually across his shoulders.

Gripping her case firmly, Livy headed to the boat. The clean-shaven Italian glanced at her, a wide smile showing off his gleaming white teeth.

"*Ciao, Signorina*. You are Miss Maclean?"

Pleased to hear him pronounce her surname correctly to rhyme with 'lane', she smiled and nodded. "*Si, Signor, grazie.*" That was about the limit of her Italian so she reverted to English. "This is my private water taxi?"

The young man's smile slipped a little as he glanced at the figure by his side. Livy realised the other man had turned around and was observing her with interest.

"Si, this is booked for you, *Signorina*, but there seems to be problem with the *signor's* booking."

"Olivia? I can't believe it is actually you!"

The cultured voice with its merest hint of accent instantly registered and Livy stared at the man properly for the first time.

"Sebastian! What are you doing here? And I'm Livy now." Of all the places in all the world came to mind.

"Hoping to board a water taxi into the Piazza San Marco, same as you it seems." His eyes crinkled in amusement.

Aware her tone had been less than friendly, Livy relaxed her shoulders. Nothing was going to spoil her first sight of Venice. "Sorry, you're the last person I expected to see here."

They appraised each other in silence until a discreet cough reminded them of their interested audience.

"You know each other? *Bene*! Maybe you share the taxi." The driver grinned even wider.

"My booking seems to have got lost in the system somewhere. Would you mind if I cadge a lift with you, Olivia?" Seb asked.

Livy contemplated him, aware he was still far too attractive to ignore, even after the three years since she'd last seen him. Of all the people in the world to have arrived here at just this moment, it had to be the one she'd never forgotten: Sebastian Leoni, six feet two of handsome hunk and major heart-breaker. And yet… those deep blue-grey eyes stirred a long-suppressed memory of how much of a couple they'd become towards the end of university in Glasgow, until they headed off in different directions. Then, after a gap of several years, they'd met again at the Scottish wedding of their mutual friend, Amy. It was as though they'd hardly been apart during the years in between, before they'd said goodbye once more.

She smiled at the young Italian to gather her thoughts and steer them away from the past. She could hardly refuse to share an empty boat since they were both going to the same destination. Besides, she was curious as to why he was in Venice.

Not answering his question directly, she finally replied. "Och, of course it would make sense to share since there's plenty of space." She caught Seb's grin at the Scottish expression he used to tease her about.

Their different worlds had collided for those few years at university until they'd parted reluctantly but never kept in touch, no matter how many promises they had made. Until that wedding where they had danced the night away and recognised how much of a spark still existed between them. Yet again, it hadn't had the opportunity to flare.

"*Bene, bene*, step on board, *signorina, signor*," the driver said, ushering them on before they changed their minds. He offered his hand to Livy and she stepped carefully onto the wooden boards, relieved she'd worn comfortable wedged shoes.

"If you sit near the back, you will see our beautiful lagoon and all the islands we pass on the way."

Making sure his passengers had sat down, the driver flashed them a wide smile and turned to collect their bags.

Once the luggage was stored in the centre of the boat, Livy sat back and tried to concentrate on their departure rather than on the man by her side. Not easy. He emanated such masculinity that her senses reacted independently to his proximity.

Their initial friendship at university, where she'd studied art history and literature while he'd concentrated on literature and journalism, had been full of promise. From the first day they met, she and Seb had an immediate connection and she was able to initiate him into Scottish culture, much to the delight of her friends. But she'd eventually stayed in Glasgow to work in the art galleries and he'd travelled the world as a hotshot journalist.

It had taken her a long time to get over him, but she'd finally acknowledged the futility of caring for someone who didn't belong in her world, nor she in his. He'd only been studying in Scotland because his Scottish mother had hoped he would be educated there. As a mark of respect for her wishes before she passed away, his father had encouraged him to go to Glasgow University.

Now, the good-looking youth had matured and broadened over the years, his black hair a bit shorter, the fine cheekbones still prominent, with the Celtic colouring of blue-grey eyes only adding to the appeal. Not that she was interested in men at the moment, even one as sexy as Sebastian. This was her time to rediscover her own hopes for the future.

"Are you ready for this, Olivia? It gets fast but is completely exhilarating." Seb broke into her thoughts.

"Ready?" She stared at his amused eyes, wondering exactly what he meant. She was ready for the journey into Venice but nothing else was on the agenda. "Absolutely. I've been told this is the best way to arrive."

"The only way," he agreed, "although it's an added pleasure sharing it with you."

Before she could summon a suitable reply, the engine roared into life and they were off, thrust into the waiting lagoon. The speed caught Livy by surprise and she inadvertently shifted position as they made a sudden right turn.

"Oops, sorry." Her hand touched Seb's and she righted herself at once.

"Don't move away on my account, Olivia." He reached out and touched her hand.

Disconcerted at his confidence, and her skin's reaction, she slipped away from him. It obviously was too long since she'd seen him if he was having this effect on her. When they'd both been invited to Amy's wedding three years ago, she'd thought this time they might have a chance together. But Sebastian had returned to his family estate in Italy to take over the wine business when his father became ill, and she was the sole carer for her mother in her final years.

Had she ever really got over him? Even the way he said her name was unlike anyone else. She decided not to remind him of the shortened form she now used.

Turning her attention to the passing scenery, Livy smiled as she caught a fleeting glimpse of the type of old Italian building she associated with Venice. Wide stretches of water interspersed with islands of various sizes as they sped across the lagoon. Livy closed her eyes and lifted her face to the blue sky, giving herself up to the sheer thrill of the ride, the breeze fingering her hair.

As the boat eventually dropped its speed a little to negotiate other water traffic, Livy was aware that Seb had slid nearer to her.

"Enjoying it, Olivia?" His voice was necessarily close to her ear so she could hear him above the noise of the speedboat.

"You were right. This is exhilarating." She laughed, caught up in the shared moment.

"You are as beautiful as ever, or even more so I believe, and I was a fool to ever let you go."

She barely caught the words and wondered if her imagination had taken flight. But the intensity of his gaze suggested he meant it and Livy had no idea how to respond. She stared down at the rushing water as unwanted memories reminded her of the last time he was this near her.

Their closeness had not gone unnoticed at the wedding when Livy had been delighted to find Seb a guest. Clever Amy had seated them together at the meal and they'd remained together all evening.

They'd even spent the next day with each other before Seb had to fly off again, once more beyond her reach. When his occasional postcard arrived, she eventually stopped reading them and their friendship withered, if not quite dying in her heart.

"Perhaps time makes fools of us all," she said at last. "Personally, I don't believe in regrets since we can't change the past." She returned his gaze but refused to respond in a flirtatious manner. For all she knew, he might already be in a happy relationship.

"Cynical these days, Olivia?" He raised an eyebrow but didn't move away.

"A realist." Watching her mother fade to a shadow before the cancer claimed her saw to that, never mind a prospective fiancé who turned out to be a monk in training or some such.

Her love of art history had kept alive her own dream of travelling to Italy one day. Since she occasionally gave lectures on the Renaissance period, Venice was the perfect excuse to combine pleasure with viewing some of the paintings in their actual setting. And here she was at last.

"I remember you always saw the glass half full," he replied. "I hope you have not changed too much. So, how long are you in Venice?"

Was it merely polite curiosity in his voice? "Unfortunately, I'm only here for three and a half days, before I pick up my cruise to Croatia and the Greek isles."

"That sounds interesting, but it does not give us long. A pity."

Livy glanced at the gleam in his eye. "Long for what?"

"For me to show you around Venice. I know it well and I'd love to introduce you to its mysteries, as you once showed me Glasgow. Or perhaps you have it all planned out?"

Since she'd been slightly wary of wandering around a strange place by herself, his offer sounded appealing. *Or was it his appeal*, a small voice whispered.

"Don't you have things to do while you're here?" she asked, while deciding on her reply.

"I'm partly on holiday this time, although I am meeting up with my sister and her husband who live here now, as well as some friends. But I would be delighted to spend a few days showing you where to go. Nothing beats watching a person's first reaction to Venezia."

Livy was glad when a call from the driver alerting them to their approach prevented any further conversation. She needed to process Seb's offer and manner, as well as her traitor body's involuntary reaction to his nearness, and the suggestion of spending time with him in this most romantic of cities.

"Keep watch, *signorina, signor,* and you will see a magnificent sight."

Livy slid across to her side of the boat so she could watch their approach. Minutes later, she gasped as the skyline took on the familiar shape of the photos she had seen of St Mark's Square from the sea. The Campanile towered into the air at one side of the piazza while the Doge's Palace spread to the right. The boat continued across the lagoon, passing a variety of other water traffic.

As they drew even closer, she caught sight of a row of gondolas along the edge of the water, then she gasped. "The Bridge of Sighs! I can't believe it's right there."

"Si, *signorina*." The young Italian grinned at her exclamation. "And soon we'll be underneath it. Your hotel is at the top of this canal."

"You've chosen well," Seb said, reminding her of his presence.

"It seems so. I wasn't sure exactly where I'd be situated." She smiled at him, aware of the unexpected pleasure of sharing her first-time arrival with him.

She watched in amazement as they sailed up the canal and under the famous bridge. Then she noticed where the water taxi was stopping and couldn't believe her luck. A genuine landing stage complete with candy-cane striped pole.

"Wow, it just gets better and better. I didn't know these were actually used outside of films," she said as she stood up.

"It is the very best way to approach a hotel on the canal, *signorina*, as long as the water level is not too high. Be careful when you step onto it," the driver said.

"Drop me here too, please, *signor*," Seb said. "I don't have far to go and I know the way." He lifted Livy's case. "I'll get that. There's a door into the hotel just ahead."

She watched the driver manoeuvre the boat around the canal, then turned to the man beside her. "It really is good to see you, Seb, and you're right, the entry to Venice was even better shared." *Even if not with a romantic partner.*

"I'm glad we met, Olivia. But you did not answer my suggestion. May I show you around while you're here?"

Aware they still stood on the landing stage, the canal water causing it to move a little now and then, Livy nodded. They were also in full view of anyone crossing a small bridge nearby and she was eager to get checked into the hotel.

"If you're sure you can spare the time, I'd like that, thanks."

"Good." He took her hand a moment before grasping the handle of her case. "I'll need to come through the hotel to get out onto the street from the main door." He grinned. "There's only one way down from here and I don't fancy a dip."

Livy laughed, realising she already was becoming more light-hearted since meeting Seb, glad she'd agreed to see him again. It was only for a few days and then their paths would diverge once more, although she didn't want to dwell on that right now.

Once inside the hotel, Seb turned to say goodbye. "Why don't I come and meet you this evening and I shall take you to dinner at a little restaurant I know. Otherwise you'll probably get lost in the dark. And that is no reflection on you. Everyone gets lost at first and it is part of the charm of Venice."

She had to admit the offer was tempting as she had no idea where to go. "That's really kind, thanks. I'd be grateful to dine out with someone who knows the city. I'd better give you my new mobile number in case you need to get in touch," she suggested.

"Good idea," Seb agreed, as they checked each other's details. "I shall see you at seven. *Ciao*, Olivia."

And he was gone, leaving her to check in and glance around the small but pleasant hotel. Fortunately, the man on duty spoke excellent English and gave her a map of Venice along with her room key.

As soon as she entered her room on the third floor, Livy knew she was going to love being here. She went straight to the window and opened the outside shutters to let the light flood in. Glancing down, she couldn't believe her luck. Below was the canal she had sailed through, under the Bridge of Sighs, and even now a gondola was negotiating its journey down it in the capable hands of the uniformed gondolier. A young couple sat close together at the back and Livy sighed. How absolutely romantic, if you had someone to share it with. But she was here to indulge quite different passions, she reminded herself.

Leaving the shutters open and the light curtain drawn across the window, her heart beat faster. She was actually here, in the most perfect city in the world for an art historian, apart from Florence perhaps. She couldn't wait to explore the narrow alleyways, the canals and bridges, and the churches that displayed as much famous art on its walls as any art gallery, from what she'd read.

She had to admit, however, that some of her increased pulse rate and excitement was due to the unexpected meeting with Seb and the forthcoming dinner on her first night in Venice. *Careful, Olivia, this is a complication you neither want nor need right now*, that voice whispered again. But surely, she could enjoy it for what it was: dinner with an old friend whom she would be saying goodbye to again? It was the thought of what might happen in between that made her stomach flip. "Absolutely nothing of any importance," she told the room, and tried to believe that was true.

Leaving the view of the canal for now, she opened her suitcase to unpack and make herself at home. Then she needed to choose an outfit befitting dinner in Venice with a sophisticated handsome escort. Hopefully, she might even have time first to go for a short wander, not too far from the hotel so she could find her way back.

As for Sebastian Leoni, she would enjoy the company of such a charming companion for a few days then they would part again as friends. Even if she lost another little bit of her heart in the process.

Chapter Two

In double quick time, Livy had unpacked half her case contents. Fortunately, she had planned ahead, packing a good selection of clothes near the top for the days in Venice. The cruise ship provided a guests' laundry room, should the need arise. Rather than waste the remainder of the afternoon light, she decided to go and explore a little before allowing enough time to choose an outfit for the evening. Besides, she could do with a coffee and cake to keep her going till dinner.

Grabbing a light shoulder bag and sunhat, she nodded to the receptionist as she found the door to the street. Since the hotel was at the top of the canal, she turned left towards the small bridge she'd noticed earlier. No doubt she'd find plenty more and she tried to take note of a landmark to guide her back the right way. The obvious one was the Bridge of Sighs; surely she wouldn't get lost if she didn't wander too far.

The narrow street led her to a wider area with shops and people, so she continued straight ahead. Her attention was immediately caught by several interesting shops on the way and she paused to stare at a window full of masks of every kind, from small discreet and pretty ones, to grotesque masks with weird nose-like protuberances, and some very fancy concoctions with lace and feathers, held by a stick. It was like a child finding a sweetie shop full of jars of edible delights and Livy planned to pay it a proper visit before leaving Venice. Next to it was a window full of beautiful Venetian silk scarves and ties in muted colours. Another must, to buy a gift for a couple friends, as well as one particularly gorgeous scarf in lilac, pink and cream swirls for herself. Perfect as a wrap for the air-conditioning on the cruise ship.

Wandering further along, she suddenly came to a halt. Without realising, she had landed right on the edge of St Mark's Square, all of it laid out before her in its wonderful familiarity from the many times she'd looked at it online and in photos. Since it was late afternoon, crowds still milled around, admiring the architecture or queuing for the Doge's Palace, Basilica or the Campanile. She would leave the palace for another day, preferably in the morning before it was quite so busy. The sound of an orchestra beckoned her on and she passed by two cafes, on opposite sides of the square, most of the tables and chairs already full. She noticed the famous Caffé Florian, possibly the most expensive one in Venice, or anywhere else. She'd need to see if her euros would stretch to that treat another day.

Passing by the Campanile towards the canal, she turned right and found another smaller café not far from the square where she could sit and watch the world pass by on the lagoon. Ordering a coffee and small almond cake, she gasped at the price even here and wondered if it was because of its view of the canal. But she was on holiday, no expense spared she reminded herself, and resolved to make the most of every second, the warmth washing over her, easing all anxiety and everyday life at home in an often-dreich Glasgow.

Smiling at anyone catching her eye as she sipped the coffee, she watched the various types of boats passing and sighed in pleasure. Was anywhere more iconic or interesting? It didn't even matter that she was alone, as it meant she could wander wherever her feet led her. A family of mother, father and two young children passed by, the wee boy and girl complaining they were tired. She guessed they'd rather be at a beach and she didn't blame them as they probably wouldn't be interested in old buildings and history.

Her thoughts finally turned again to Seb and the forthcoming dinner. Now revived by the coffee and lulled into a soporific relaxation by the pleasure of sitting near the famous canal, her stomach flipped when she pictured him beside her on the water taxi. How could he have such an effect on her after all this time? Yet she couldn't forget the day they had parted for the second time, the way his lips had seared hers as though claiming her for always.

A fanciful suggestion, she knew now, but their connection had been as complete as any, without the complication of sex. She'd sometimes wondered if it was too platonic and that was why they hadn't made more effort to keep in touch. It was as though they'd held back from that ultimate intimacy while neither was free to offer commitment.

As she mused on her unexpected meeting, Livy watched a long white and yellow boat passing along the canal, filled with tourists. That must be the vaporetto she'd read about, high on her list of essential experiences.

She checked the time to find the afternoon almost gone. Reluctantly, she vacated her seat by the canal and wandered back through St Mark's Square, or the piazza perhaps she should call it. Plenty of people still lingering at the cafés, she noticed, and why not since they'd paid handsomely for the privilege. Besides, the orchestra was worth listening to and she wasn't the only passer-by to pause.

Trying not to be too obvious, she glanced in appreciation at the famous Caffé Florian, resolving to visit it before her short break here was over. Then she noticed a man and woman sitting side by side at one of the small tables, engrossed in their conversation.

Her breath caught. Seb with a glamorous brunette, both elegant, oozing sophistication. Livy quickened her steps before he saw her and soon she was at the top of the square, disoriented for a moment, trying to remember which way to turn.

Standing in front of a window full of masks, she tried to gather herself. But seeing Seb there, so natural in that environment, reminded Livy again of their very different backgrounds and lives. She would never be that elegant, her five-foot four stature and straight chestnut hair more homely than glamorous, which didn't bother her at all in Scotland. But seeing Seb with another woman warned her not to allow her heart to be stirred too much by him. It didn't work the first or second time, so why should now be any different?

When she reached the end of the street with shops, Livy hesitated. How did she get back to the hotel? She didn't remember coming through such a narrow alley. Then she caught sight of a small bridge over a canal and headed towards it. Glancing to her right, she saw the Bridge of Sighs at the end of the canal, so she only had to cross this small bridge and the hotel was a few yards on.

What a great landmark to stop her getting lost, as far as St Mark's at least, and she was grateful again that Seb was taking her to dinner on her first evening, though some of the pleasure had dissipated after seeing him with that elegant woman. It might be his sister, of course, or one of his friends, but it didn't change the fact that she didn't belong in his world for more than a few days holiday. But she still aimed to make the most of her evening out and hoped she had an outfit worthy of it.

Two hours later, Livy surveyed herself in the wardrobe mirror. Not perfect, which she never would be, but passable. Thankfully, she'd bought a couple of new dresses for her holiday and the one she now wore felt right. Silky in swirls of lilac and pink, it floated to just below the knee. A pair of pink and cream sling backs completed the look and she added a fine wool cream wrap for the cooler evening. A slick of pink lipstick and flick of mascara, hair gleaming from the shower and blow dry, and she was as ready as ever.

Seb had seen her in all kinds of casual wear at university, then glammed up for a wedding, but she admitted she wanted to impress him a little, especially when he was more used to sophisticated Italian women who always knew exactly how to dress.

She was studying a map on the wall of the hotel lobby when Seb arrived. Casual but head-turning in smart dark trousers and an open-neck shirt in a deep cobalt blue that enhanced his eyes and black hair. Her heart reacted at once, though she only smiled and accepted his kiss on both cheeks.

"*Ciao*, Olivia, *bella*," he said, the Italian compliment waking the butterflies in her abdomen. "That's a lovely dress for a lovely lady."

"*Grazie*." She was determined to keep it light-hearted. "You scrub up well yourself."

He laughed as he took her arm, escorting her from the hotel. Venice was alive in a different way at night, the day trippers gone back to their cruise ships, the locals and residents ready to socialise for the evening.

Even the bridges looked more romantic with couples strolling arm in arm, like they did too, but not in quite the same way. "How beautiful in this soft light." Livy sighed. "I think I like it even more at night."

"Many people do, not least because many of the tourists have gone." He squeezed her hand. "Not the kind that actually *stay* here for a few days, of course."

As they wandered along, through a couple of narrower streets, over another bridge, Livy was thankful again for a companion who knew exactly where he was going. She was completely lost already and would never find her way back on her own. She really would need to wander around in daylight to get her bearings.

"It's along this next street," Seb said. "One of my favourite places."

It was obvious he was known to the owner who greeted him personally with a handshake.

"Your table is ready, Signor Leoni. *Buona sera, signorina.*" He bowed briefly over Livy's hand.

Feeling like an honoured guest, Livy glanced around as they sat at a discreetly positioned, intimate table for two. Much as she appreciated every moment, a little niggle of doubt crept in. Wasn't this a little too intimate?

As the evening progressed, however, Livy forgot her doubts, enjoying the surroundings, the food and most of all the attention of the handsome man across from her. Let tomorrow take care of itself.

Satiated with the excellent fish, wine and company, Livy was happy to stroll down to St Mark's with Seb, before returning to the hotel. Although not as densely busy as daytime, there was a friendly buzz about the piazza, with a few vendors offering paintings of Venice or children's Pinocchio toys. Music filled the air from one of the cafés and Livy sighed in contentment.

"Happy?" Seb asked, linking arms.

"Very. It's a dream come true being here at last." She didn't add how much he was adding to the experience.

"I think you will want to return even after a few days here."

They wandered down to the canal and along past the Bridge of Sighs, a row of dark gondolas moored on the still water. She had read they were overpriced but she might treat herself one evening, since she was sparing no expense, although it wouldn't be the same on her own.

After walking a little further, they stood on one of the small bridges and Livy stared at the water below before glancing up at her companion.

"Thank you for this evening, Seb. You've made my first day so much more wonderful."

They were standing very close and he leaned nearer to kiss her cheek. "I'm glad we met again, Olivia. It was a pleasure to dine together. Perhaps you are tired now after travelling?"

Much as she didn't want the evening to end, she was aware he might be going on somewhere else. And he was right, not only was she tired but she needed lots of energy for the next few days to walk around Venice.

She nodded. "I think it's time for bed." As soon as the words were out, she was glad of the darkness that hid her embarrassment.

Seb laughed. "Then I shall escort you back to your hotel, *signorina*."

She had no idea how they got to the door from where they'd been and again she was grateful for Seb's presence. Time to find her own way about tomorrow.

"May I offer a suggestion, Olivia?" Seb asked, continuing when she nodded. "If you wish to acquaint yourself with much of the area around the Grand Canal, I recommend you take the number one vaporetto which will transport you right up the canal. Either you can stay on board and enjoy the sights, or you can get off whenever you like and walk part of the way back."

"That sounds perfect." Even though she was unexpectedly disappointed that Seb would not be with her. "I need to get my bearings."

"Don't worry if you get lost, you will eventually find your way to the piazza. And try to sit at the front of the boat so you can take photos, if you wish."

"I'm looking forward to it. Thanks again for making my first evening so enjoyable, Seb."

"As I said, it was my pleasure. Dining is much better with company, so I would be delighted if you will dine with me again tomorrow evening and you can tell me about your day."

Surprised he had the time and inclination, she smiled. "I hope you're not cancelling any prior arrangements on my behalf."

"Not at all, and I want to continue our reunion."

Since the tiny flutter in her abdomen proved how much she wanted that too, she agreed. "Then I'll very much look forward to it, thanks."

He put his hands on her shoulders and for a moment she imagined he was about to kiss her properly, but he pecked both her cheeks. "Goodnight, Olivia, and sleep well on your first night."

She watched him stroll in the direction of the piazza before seeking her room. She immediately went across to the window to peer down at the canal and her evening was complete when a gondola came into view, a couple reclining, arms around each other, while the gondolier was singing! She wrapped her arms around her body as she watched, smiling that such a cliché turned out to be real.

Closing the shutters eventually, she tried to quell her excitement at exploring on her own tomorrow then having the pleasure of such a dining companion again. Already a little bit of her heart was in love with Venice. *And that's as far as it goes*, her small voice of reason whispered. Sebastian Leoni was not on the menu except as a very pleasant interlude to real life.

Chapter Three

When she stepped out of the hotel next morning, Livy smiled at everything around her, almost believing that the gondolier singing last night had been a dream. She had slept well then enjoyed the light breakfast of fruit and a croissant in the small friendly dining room. But today was all about exploring this city on the water.

At least she knew how to get down to the canal where she could catch a vaporetto, although there was no direct route from the hotel except to cross a small bridge then find her way to St Mark's square. Easier in daylight and she recognised a few of the shops she'd passed before. She suspected the piazza was always this busy during the day and she wandered past the cafés already filling with morning coffee drinkers. She had resolved to follow Seb's advice and see the main part of Venice from the Grand Canal.

Scanning the notice where the boats stopped, Livy found she could catch the number one vaporetto here, so bought a ticket for several days and joined the people already waiting. It was only a few minutes before the long boat appeared and she went straight to the front to claim one of the seats. Just as well she'd ventured out early as it would only get busier.

From the moment they sailed off from the edge, Livy was captivated by the sights. The canal itself was busy with all kinds of water traffic but her eyes went immediately to the buildings on each side. Some in various states of repair, others the grand old palaces of several centuries ago where the aristocracy had lived, many now containing apartments for those lucky enough to afford a view of the canal. A profusion of flower-filled window boxes and small wrought-iron balconies adorned many of them, and everything looked exactly as she'd imagined.

Making sure her camera was secure as she perched on the edge of her seat, Livy snapped as much as she could, hoping to find out more about some of the buildings later. As they negotiated a small bend, she sat stunned by the vista opening out before her: a whole stretch of the Grand Canal with gracious buildings on either side, cafés along one narrow walkway, landing stages for gondolas and water taxis with the candy cane poles, wherever there was no walking path. Then up ahead, she saw a well-known attraction in tourist guides: the famous Rialto Bridge. She hadn't realised that part of it was quite so covered in and was longing to walk across it. She had already planned to take the vaporetto to the furthest point then get off and stroll all the way back, stopping for food, drink and browsing on the way. She had all day, the sun was already shining, and this was one of the best ways to explore the heart of Venice.

They had stopped at various stages to take on more passengers and Livy put her camera away to enjoy the final part of the sail without being distracted, sliding up her seat to allow an elderly couple to sit down beside her.

"Thanks, love," the woman said. "We never tire of seeing this, do we, Fred? It's a bit different from England." She nudged her husband. He grinned and shook his head but didn't say anything.

"Have you been often?" Livy asked, thankful she'd already seen enough of the canal side for this first sail on it. The elderly lady obviously hoped for a wee chat.

"We came here for our honeymoon, then our silver anniversary. And now it's our golden, though I don't know where those fifty years have gone."

"Oh, that's lovely. I can understand why you wanted to return. It's my first time here and I love it already."

The woman's smile slipped for a moment. "You enjoy every minute, love. I think this will be our last visit. Fred's memory is beginning to go, and I reckon this is our swan song in a way. But we've had a happy life together and no regrets."

Livy blinked away the threat of a tear. She patted the woman's hand. "Well I hope you have a wonderful time while you're here."

Fred continued to smile, and Livy guessed he was content for now. It reminded her how cruel the most advanced form of Alzheimer's could be, and she hoped it wouldn't get that bad for the couple.

"Thanks, dear. And I hope you find your own happy life with someone. Well, this is our stop. Bye, love."

Livy watched the couple step onto the walkway, the wife carefully holding her husband's hand, directing his feet. She waved as the boat carried on to her stop. At least the couple had been lucky enough to find a life partner.

She wasn't surprised that people returned here at special times in their lives. It certainly wouldn't be her only visit, whether or not she'd have to come alone again. Most of her friends were in a relationship, married with children, or unable to take the same holidays. As it turned out, it was better to be on her own to wander at will, not to mention dinner 'a deux' with Seb for which she was grateful. Evening must be the worst time of day to be alone in a strange city.

When the vaporetto pulled into the next stop, Livy shelved all other thoughts and stepped down to the quayside. Time to explore. She noticed the Rialto Bridge wasn't too far back but soon found no easy way to reach it. The path beside the canal only went so far before turning up to the inner streets and alleyways. It was the same further along; impossible to walk in a straight route beside the water. She took out the little map from the hotel but after peering at it this way and that, she put it back in her bag. It was easier, and possibly more fun, to see where her feet took her.

Reflecting that it was probably what made Venice so interesting, not knowing where you might end up or what you'd find on the way, Livy smiled in contentment, pleased she had all day to enjoy exploring. No agenda, timetable or definite plans – a complete change from her normal busy life.

She noticed a couple of cafés at the first square she came to, the tables and chairs already outside to welcome passers-by. Although it had no view of the water, she could watch the world go by while sipping a coffee in the warmth of the Italian morning.

"*Ciao, signorina,*" a middle-aged waiter approached, charm oozing from him like most of the Italian males, no matter their age.

"*Ciao, signor. Un cappuccino, per favore,*" she managed, since that would be one of her most used phrases while here.

He smiled at her effort as though pleased she had tried and he'd hardly gone inside when he returned with a glass of water for her. She liked this kind gesture at the cafés, though didn't intend trying the tiny strong espresso it usually accompanied. Not unless it was after an evening meal, at which time she understood that milky coffee was frowned upon in Italy.

"*Grazi*e," she said and received another half nod and wide grin in return.

She was pleased to find a little almond biscotti on the saucer with her coffee; perfect. Livy sighed in pleasure as she turned her chair to the sun, sunglasses allowing her to watch the people going by and to look around at the old buildings and small fountain in the middle of the square. It was so Italian, yet somehow Venetian with its own unique identity.

When she eventually decided to move, the waiter paused as he took her payment.

"You are Eenglish?" he asked in a thick accent.

"Scottish," she replied, wondering if he'd get the difference.

"Ah, *si*, Scotland," he nodded in delight. "My uncle, he live there."

At such coincidence, his smile widened and Livy hoped he wasn't going to ask if she knew him. People often misunderstood how big a country it was with hundreds of miles between areas. But his next words were a suggestion.

"You see marble church. Not far, up street, over bridge."

His English seemed to give out and Livy nodded. "*Grazie. Ciao, signor.*"

To please the friendly man, Livy headed up the narrow street to the left of the square, turning once to wave before the waiter went to serve someone else.

As usual, the streets became narrower and some crossed a canal topped with a bridge, but Livy couldn't see any sign of a church. She shrugged, continuing to stroll past old apartments, the brickwork a dark sandstone pink in the morning sun, some with washing strung across a balcony, and no sign of any shops. Then she paused as she neared another small bridge. And there, just beyond the other side of it was what looked like a church, although a much lighter colour than most. Surely that must be the one mentioned?

Once over the bridge, Livy stood before the stunning building that was bordered on one side by the canal. From her knowledge of architecture, it appeared to be Renaissance style, its arches and panels highly decorated in what looked like off-white marble. She'd never seen anything like it and only hoped it was open so she could find out more about it.

Pushing the rather plain door, she let out a breath of gratitude when it opened. Inside, the marble continued around all the walls and front of the church. Then she looked up to see the whole barrel-vaulted ceiling covered in small paintings, each in its own panel.

She suddenly became aware of a young man sitting at a table opposite the door and she smiled. "This is beautiful."

He nodded in agreement. "It is very special, the *Santa Maria de Miracoli*. You can read about it here." He offered her a laminated sheet of paper with details in English. "Please, you can look and sit down if you wish."

"*Grazie*." Livy was so overwhelmed by the beauty of it all that it was only when she wandered over to sit on a pew that she noticed the church was in fact quite simple otherwise, as though the marble and the art-covered ceiling were enough distraction to worship. The pews were wooden and the focus of those sitting in them would be completely on the altar piece of the virgin and child on the raised part of the single nave, reached by red-carpeted steps.

She was pleased no other tourists had found their way here yet, as it added to the feeling of awe to sit on her own and contemplate such fine architecture and art mingled with spirituality. She wasn't particularly religious but was always aware of something other than the mundane reality of life, reinforced by her mother's faith that death was not the end though her mortal body had given out.

Eventually, she read a little of the information and was not surprised to learn the building had been completed in 1489 and was indeed a fine example of Venetian Renaissance art. The painting of the Virgin and child, which had been commissioned at the beginning of the 1400s, was originally placed in a tabernacle at the patron's house. After the painting elicited vast public devotion, and subsequently was deemed miraculous, this wonderful church was eventually built to house it in more fitting surroundings.

She gazed up again at the amazing panels of art in the vaulted ceiling: fifty of them depicting prophets and patriarchs, painted by Pennacchi and his contemporaries. According to the information, other work was most likely by Lombardi who had planned this architectural masterpiece of marbled beauty.

By the time she thanked the young man and left the church, Livy had to shield her eyes from the bright sun. Taking a photograph of the whole exterior proved difficult because of the canal at one side but she did her best as it was such a unique example of 15th century Venetian art. She wasn't surprised it was a popular venue for weddings as it resembled a huge carved ivory box, with exquisitely detailed crosses, arches and a beautiful rose window.

She continued up the street ahead, with no idea of where she was and soon came to other narrow lanes crossing in both directions. Reminding herself it was all part of the pleasure of wandering through the streets of Venice, she turned to the right. Hopefully, that should eventually take her back in the direction of St Mark's.

The further Livy wandered, the more lost she became and she tried to quell her rising anxiety. Surely, she would find the right direction at some point? She had turned along yet another narrow alley when her attention was caught by an interesting shop window. It seemed to be a kind of stationers but with unusual items. When she opened the door, she noticed the small interior, one man standing behind the counter engrossed in whatever he was doing.

"*Buon giorno, signorina*," he said, glancing up with a smile. "How may I assist you?"

Since she had no idea, Livy smiled and asked if she could look at the notebooks displayed in a glass case below the counter. At least she presumed that was their purpose. The covers were beautifully designed in different swirls of colour and she wanted to see inside them.

Like the other locals she had spoken to, the man was friendly with a barely detectable accent.

"All of our work has this marble effect. It is a special hand-made process and as you see, it produces pretty effects."

Livy opened one of the small hardback books to find good quality cream paper inside. "This is lovely. I would like two of this size, please. The red with brown, and this colourful pattern of blues and purples."

They were a little more expensive than ordinary notebooks but that was to be expected for such gorgeous craftsmanship. They were an ideal size for a handbag, useful while travelling around.

"*Grazie, signorina*. I shall wrap them for you?"

"*Si, grazie, signor.*" She was enjoying practising her accent and resolved to learn a few more Italian words and phrases before leaving.

Carrying her purchases in the pretty small bag with the shop's logo, Livy understood why it was best to wander these many streets without an agenda, since there were interesting shops to discover along the way.

As she passed another open square, she noticed a sign on a corner wall with an arrow pointing towards St Mark's. At least she might find other signs now and then. Noting a few people already taking seats at the cafés, she wandered over to the prettiest and sat at a table for two on the concourse. A quick glance at the menu assured her of an acceptable light lunch.

She was at the coffee stage, watching the many tourists wandering by when she noticed one particular couple. Sebastian and that woman again, this time strolling along arm in arm on the other side of the square. Picking up the menu to shield her face, Livy studied them without being seen. *Who was she?*

With a jolt of self-awareness, she knew it mattered. Now that he'd come back into her life, she wanted to enjoy every minute with him but not if he was in a relationship. Waiting until they were well gone, she paid the waiter and wandered across the square.

A large poster caught her eye. A concert of Vivaldi music that evening at one of the churches near her hotel. How she would love to hear that, but the tickets would probably be gone by now.

The rest of the afternoon passed in a blur of narrow streets, busy squares, mask shops, and always hordes of tourists, especially around St Mark's. Instead of heading to the hotel, she strolled past the Bridge of Sighs, stopping on the footbridge beside the lagoon to take a photo of it straight on. Such a poignant name for the covered passage through which condemned prisoners had taken their final steps, its ornate white limestone containing tiny lattice-style windows which might have offered them a glimpse of the canal.

Carrying on, she eventually reached a quieter part. She knew from her guide book and map that the Arsenale, the old Venetian shipyards area, was situated here. She noticed the large brown building guarded by white lions and statues, with a tall clock tower on either side of the wooden bridge. Although a naval museum stood by, Livy gave it a miss, content just to wander where she could.

It was peaceful strolling around this part, with a good path alongside the water, away from the busyness. A long River Cruise boat was moored alongside the path; far more discreet than the monstrously huge cruise ships that polluted the water at times. She'd read, however, that the city was limiting the areas where the ships could enter. Her own ship was a much smaller one with only several hundred people on board rather than the thousands on the mega ships. Not that she felt quite the same excitement for the cruise. Something to do with meeting Seb, perhaps?

By the time she returned to the hotel, Livy was exhausted with all the walking. A warm bath was called for before getting ready for her dinner date with Seb. The flutter of excitement in her abdomen told her how much she welcomed his company, even after seeing him twice with that other woman. And it wasn't only because she didn't want to eat alone.

She'd hardly reached her room when she heard a text message ping on her mobile. Seb. For a moment, disappointment coursed through her at the thought he was going to cancel. But she couldn't believe it when she read the message.

\>Hi – how about a Vivaldi concert this evening. Have tickets. Call me. Seb x<

Was he psychic? How strange that she'd just been looking at that poster today. Perhaps he'd seen it too when walking past it. He also knew she liked that type of music. She called him right away.

"Hi, Seb. Got your text. That would be fantastic, thanks."

"I guessed you might enjoy it in the composer's own city. It's at eight o'clock so how about an early dinner then we could have a nightcap afterwards."

"Perfect. Just about to soak my weary limbs after a day exploring."

"Pick you up in an hour and you can tell me all about it. There's a restaurant next door to the concert."

The day had suddenly become even better, Livy reflected as she sank into a bath full of the fragrant oil the hotel provided. At least he wanted to take *her* to the concert and not the mysterious woman he'd been seeing. She would accept his company for as long as it was available then wave goodbye with no regrets at the end of her Venetian interlude. Or so she promised herself.

Chapter Four

It was another warm evening and Livy was grateful for the dressier clothes she'd brought for the cruise, although she hadn't expected to need so many of them in Venice.

As promised, the restaurant was right next to the venue where the concert was being held. She hadn't realised both were along the side of the lagoon, with a wonderful view across to the island of San Giorgio and its magnificent white-fronted church and tall campanile.

"Have you tried the local wine, Valpolicella?" Seb asked. "Good, not too strong."

"No, but I'd like to, please. When in Venice and all that." Then Livy frowned. "Surely there are no vineyards here?"

"Valpolicella is the beautiful wine-growing area in the hills near Verona, worth a day trip to both the next time you are here."

"Now, there's a lovely idea." Livy was quite sure there would be a next time, although it would never be the same without Seb.

He was right, the wine complemented their pork and polenta meal very well and the large hotel restaurant was relaxing, if not as intimate as the previous evening.

"I can't believe you managed to get tickets to the concert," Livy said during coffee. "I was looking at a poster for it today, wishing I could go."

"Telepathy," Seb joked. "And a good memory of our time together in Glasgow."

She remembered their evenings out to concerts and cafés, glad he did too. She almost mentioned seeing him with a companion but decided it was none of her business, or it shouldn't be. Maybe that was when he'd seen the poster.

When she mentioned visiting the marble church, he knew it at once.

"A very popular venue for weddings, as you can imagine. Did you walk over the Rialto Bridge since it is near?"

"Not yet. I took the Vaporetto right up the canal as you suggested but got lost in all the narrow streets and over various bridges after getting off. A kind café owner told me to go and see the pretty church."

Seb laughed. "That's the magic of Venice – you never know where you'll end up or what you'll find on the way. Perhaps you would like to visit the Accademia Gallery, the finest collection of pre-19th century paintings? Or do you get enough of art at home?"

"No, I never tire of it and of course I must visit. I suspect I won't have enough time on this trip to do everything."

"I have a suggestion for tomorrow, if you haven't planned your day yet. Why don't we spend part of it together and I'll lead you to some of the places you want to see."

Much as she'd enjoyed wandering around on her own, a surge of pleasure told her she would rather have his company. "If you have time then I'll happily accept. I'll make you a list." At his expression, she laughed. "Only joking. The art gallery and Rialto would be great."

They were in a light-hearted mood when it was time for the concert and Livy couldn't fail to notice the admiring glances a few women sent Seb's way when they got up to leave. She'd been used to that reaction in Glasgow everywhere they went, but it was gratifying to find him equally admired here.

The church hosting the concert was only a few steps along and already dusk was approaching, the water traffic lessening on the still lagoon. Their seats were perfectly placed to view the orchestra at the front and Livy's anticipation grew as they tuned up.

Seb touched her hand for a moment and she smiled, pleased to be sharing it with him. The outside of the church was off-white and nothing special but inside it was more sumptuous, almost like a grand concert hall. Livy's attention went straight to the magnificent paintings and frescoes on the walls, as well as the beautiful altar beneath which members of the orchestra were tuning their instruments.

As the first notes echoed around the old building, Livy closed her eyes, letting the music envelop her senses. Although the *Four Seasons* was probably Vivaldi's most well-known piece, she enjoyed most Baroque music and was pleased to find a varied programme.

At the interval, they stayed in their seats allowing Livy to absorb the church's atmosphere.

"Did you know that *La Chiesa della Pieta'* is the very church in which Antonio Vivaldi lived and composed for a time?" Seb asked.

"No, I hadn't realised that. What an ideal venue in which to enjoy the composer's work." She closed her eyes to imagine the eighteenth-century audience in their grand gowns, wigs and fine clothes.

Once the final notes of the second half had faded into the high ceiling, Livy sighed. "That was wonderful, Seb. Thank you."

He squeezed her hand, smiling into her eyes. "As always, it was a pleasure to share it with you, Olivia."

The night air was still balmy, twilight now descended, casting a mysterious midnight blue sheen across the lagoon, several moored gondolas dark along its edge. Livy had no problem imagining the masked revellers amongst the alleys and bridges during the carnival and hoped she might experience it herself one day.

"Nightcap?" Seb asked, as they strolled along the water side.

"Absolutely." She didn't want the evening to end yet, the music still thrumming through her, Venice seeping into her soul, Sebastian by her side.

"Have you heard of Harry's Bar?" Seb asked, before she got carried away with the direction of her thoughts.

"Oh, yes, I'd forgotten it was in Venice. Famous for the Bellini, whatever that is exactly."

"That's the one, although the bar is nothing special really, apart from its famous clientele and the prices. But it would be a pity not to visit while you are here."

"I'm happy with that, if you are."

"It's not far along past San Marco."

It seemed completely natural to stroll hand in hand. A bitter sweet experience, Livy decided, to be in this man's company yet to know it was for so short a time again. It had been bad enough saying goodbye the last time after their friend's wedding, but to meet so unexpectedly these years later seemed like fate. Was it mocking them?

The sign for Harry's Bar was so discreet, on the glass door of a grey building, that she would probably have walked by not realising it was there. She discovered it had been in existence since the early 1930s and inside it retained some of the old-fashioned ambience, yet with a modern vibe. Finding a small table at the side, they sat down to absorb the buzz of conversation.

"I imagined we'd be sitting at a bar," Livy said, "but this way I can people watch."

"There's a restaurant upstairs but this is where some of the famous names from the past would be found: Hemingway, Orson Welles, Hitchcock, and more recent celebrities."

"Must have been wonderful to be part of it in those days, before the hordes of tourists arrived," Livy mused.

"It's mostly locals catching up with each other by this time in the evening," Seb said.

As if to prove his words, a well-dressed couple entered and waved to another couple already seated.

"I don't believe this," Seb said, standing up as the man and woman neared their table while Livy watched with interest.

"Isabella? And Luca, *ciao*! You must meet my friend, Olivia." He turned to Livy. "This is my bossy sister and her patient husband."

Livy stood so she didn't feel at a disadvantage as she took in the handsome couple's elegant, stylish clothes.

"*Ciao*, Olivia," Isabella said. "I have heard so much about you and it is good to meet at last."

Livy couldn't have been more warmly greeted, when Isabella and Luca kissed her cheeks. "I'm pleased to meet you both," she said.

"We must join our friends who are waiting but I hope you will come to the party tomorrow evening. Promise you will bring Olivia, Sebastian."

Isabella's command brooked no argument and Seb nodded. "Of course, if Olivia agrees."

Since it was taken out of her hands, Livy laughed. "I would love to see you again, thank you."

"And now, I'm about to introduce her to the famous Bellini," Seb said, kissing his sister before sitting down again.

"Enjoy," Isabella said, her eyes alight with speculation as she smiled at Livy, her husband merely flashing her a wide smile.

Once the couple had joined their friends, Seb took Livy's hand. "I apologise for my sister's exuberance, but she's been hoping to meet you."

"I like her," Livy said, wondering when they'd been talking about her.

"First things first. Shall I order our Bellinis?"

"Absolutely. Can't wait to try it."

When she took her first cool sip, Livy tasted the peach blended with the Prosecco. "Mm, delicious and refreshing."

"It is made to an exact recipe, originating with a previous member of the Cipriani family. To be authentic, it must use pureed white peach juice; nothing else will do."

"And the name? Is it after the famous Venetian artist by any chance?"

"But of course." Seb smiled. "The shade of pink is supposed to resemble the saint's toga in one of the artist's paintings."

As Livy sipped her cold drink, appreciating every last fragrant drop, she watched the various people arriving until all the seats were taken, even the stools at the bar.

"Is it always this busy?" she asked.

"No doubt it must vary but it's always been like this when I've visited. Are you enjoying it?"

"Love it. It kind of reminds me of some of the trendier places in Glasgow, for the friendly atmosphere, though not the setting, obviously."

"I remember a few of those." Seb took her hand, hesitating as though choosing his words carefully. "I've missed you, Olivia."

At first, she wasn't sure she'd heard properly as laughter sounded from a nearby table. But the intensity of his gaze made her pulse quicken.

"I've missed you too, Seb, but our worlds have diverged since those university days."

"Much to my regret, Olivia. Yet, I cannot believe you are here in Venice on your own and not with an adoring lover."

Raising her eyes at his direct observation, she shrugged. "Turned out the last one preferred to travel alone, and maybe I do too." She added that bit lest he think she was pining after someone else. He wasn't exactly forthcoming about his own situation.

"What about you? Wife? Children? Adoring girlfriend?" *Who was that elegant woman?*

He grinned. "Not recently. What a sad couple we are."

Nodding her head, she returned his gaze. They were hardly a couple. Had she understood his unspoken meaning - the waste of years searching for the perfect other? All the time, she was aware deep inside that there had only ever been this one person who made her heart leap at his nearness. And he'd always been out of reach.

"So, where do we go from here?" she asked, allowing him to interpret it however he chose.

He glanced at their clasped hands before looking up with a grin. "For now, I suggest a stroll back along by the lagoon, whenever you wish to leave."

Doubtless, he understood her deeper meaning but he was right to lighten their conversation. They'd been forced into rekindling their friendship for the third time by the unexpected meeting. How could it become anything more?

"Ready when you are," Livy said, suddenly wanting to be in the open, away from all the jollity of Harry's Bar.

When they stood up, Isabella caught their attention and waved them over. "Remember about the party, Sebastian. I look forward to seeing you again, Olivia."

Seb kissed his sister's cheek and waved to the others at the table, before steering Livy towards the door.

"You've had a long day, *cara mia*, and you need some energy for tomorrow."

Stifling a yawn, Livy had to agree. She had the next day to look forward to Seb's company as well as an evening party. How could she have imagined that her few days in Venice would be quite so exciting?

The evening atmosphere was so different from day time, the glistening lagoon dark as they strolled along, each deep in thought. The domed roof of San Giorgio loomed high in the distance on the other side, while the buildings they passed belonged to another period, a time of Casanova, and Bellini, Byron, and masked balls.

When Seb put his arm around her shoulder, she didn't move away, remembering other times when it had seemed so natural. They wandered up through St Mark's and eventually to the little bridge that led across to her hotel. Pausing in the centre for a moment, they watched a gondola sail beneath, transporting a couple too engrossed in each other to notice them.

"Could anything be more romantic?" she whispered.

"Only if you are with a special person," Seb replied.

They stared at each other, neither speaking, then he bent his head and his lips touched hers. It was hardly a kiss, yet Livy's pulse quickened before they parted. She took his proffered hand as they continued to the hotel, not sure if she was glad the moment had been so brief, or disappointed it wasn't a proper kiss.

At the door of the hotel, he merely pecked her cheeks before bidding her goodnight.

"Thanks for a wonderful evening, Seb."

"My pleasure, *cara mia*. Sleep well and I shall see you tomorrow."

Before going to bed, Livy stared out of the window at the now silent, empty canal below. That was twice he had used the Italian for my dear, or my darling, but which had he meant? It was only as she put down her unread book that she remembered the woman she'd seen him with twice since she arrived. And she was not his sister.

Chapter Five

They had arranged to meet at the vaporetto stop nearest to St Mark's the next morning. The weather had been kind so far and today was no different. At least there was no threat of the heavy rain that sometimes caused so much flooding for this city on the lagoon.

Dressed in a comfortable cotton skirt, t-shirt and flat shoes, Livy had a quick fruit and yoghurt breakfast before heading to the water side. Today, she was partly wearing her 'art historian hat', one of the reasons Venice had attracted her in the first place. So many of the churches had work by Tintoretto, Bellini, Titian and others that the whole city was virtually an art gallery.

Seb was already leaning against the railing when she arrived and she observed him unseen for a few moments as she approached. Along with his lean frame and black hair, he exuded elegance as only certain Italian men could, yet his deep blue-grey eyes were his Scottish mother's legacy, creating that more Celtic appearance at times. A lethal combination to many women as Livy had discovered since university days. Why then had he not married by now?

He turned when she was within speaking distance, as though aware of her approach, and she noticed the smile that crinkled the corners of his eyes.

"*Ciao*, Olivia. It's another beautiful day to explore."

"Morning, Seb. Hope I didn't keep you waiting."

"Not at all. Our transport is almost here."

Since many of the day trippers hadn't yet arrived, they found perfect seats to view their sail along the Grand Canal.

"I love those old buildings," Livy said, as they passed one with particularly ornate architecture of arches and small balconies.

"That's the Gothic *Ca' D'Oro*, the House of Gold, on our right which contains a few Titians and Tintorettos, including the painting of my named saint, Sebastian. Many of the buildings such as this were palaces at one time, although some are now hotels, or apartments, or government offices."

"What's the huge octagonal church on the other side?" Livy decided to make the most of her personal guide while she had the chance.

"Ah, the *Santa Maria Della Salute* heralds the entrance to the Grand Canal. A stunning baroque building that is over three hundred years old. In that one, you'll find more Titians, plus Tintoretto's *Marriage at Cana*."

"It's hard to imagine so many famous works of art displayed in churches." Livy could see that she'd need more than these few days to explore Venice, if she were to include every church of interest. A good excuse to return.

As they sailed further along the canal, she remembered something she'd read. "Didn't George Clooney get married here a few years ago?"

Seb grinned at her change of focus. "I believe so. I'll point out the venue as we go past."

Livy had seen many paintings, photos and films set in Venice, but it was quite different actually being here, sailing up the famous canal with her handsome escort. It was such a timeless place, scarcely changed since the fourteenth and fifteenth centuries when it was one of the most important trading cities in Europe.

"We're almost at the wedding reception venue of Clooney if you're interested." Seb brought her back to the present and she followed his gaze to the opulent greyish white palazzo that had hosted the famous couple and their guests.

"Must have been quite a party," Livy said, suitably impressed at anyone being married in this romantic city. "That reminds me, where exactly is the party this evening?" she asked as they headed towards the Rialto.

"At Isabella and Luca's apartment. My sister enjoys any excuse to gather people around her. Don't worry, I shall escort you there. I'm lodging with them while here."

Livy smiled, looking forward to it. The cruise was going to seem very lonely after these few whirlwind days. But she'd face that when it arrived.

"We can get off at the Accademia Bridge and visit the gallery first, if that suits you. They allow fewer than two hundred people in at the one time, so it is better to get there early," Seb suggested. "Then we can walk back and stop at the Rialto."

"Sounds perfect," she agreed.

When he took her hand while she stepped down from the boat, she kept it in his as they strolled along. Like so many other couples, she reflected, or lovers. The thought warmed her face and she looked around as she reined in her imagination. How many times had she pictured a more permanent relationship with Sebastian, only to face yet another inevitable parting. This time would be no different, except that another piece of her heart belonged to him.

The Accademia was situated at the foot of the Academy Bridge, not surprisingly, and resembled a huge church on the outside. By the time they had investigated what was displayed in each of the twenty-four rooms, Livy had decided to concentrate on viewing some of the most well-known paintings. Room ten was one of the most interesting, containing Veronese's *Feast in the House of Levi*, Tintoretto's *Transport of the Body of St Mark*, plus Titian's final work, *Pietà*.

"There's only one painting by Canaletto, in room seventeen," Livy read. "And I'd love to visit room twenty for the Bellini and the Carpaccio paintings."

"Take your time and view whatever you want," Seb said. "I haven't seen most of them yet."

Reassured, Livy stood in awe before the famous Bellini painting, *Procession of the Cross in the Piazza San Marco*, appreciating the detail of the Doge and members of Venetian political life, along with friars and priests, watched at either side by crowds from all Venetian society. How little of the square had changed since all those centuries ago.

Another that held her attention was the huge colourful *Feast in the House of Levi* by Veronese. It immediately reminded her of depictions of the Last Supper, although this was a far more decadent display of a feast and when she mentioned it to Seb, he nodded.

"I have heard of this one. It was indeed originally named *Last Supper*, but the Inquisition objected and Veronese merely changed the name, although it is sometimes known as *Christ in the House of Levi*."

Livy smiled. She couldn't imagine it had fooled anyone who viewed it. The Christ-like figure sat at the middle of the table conversing with the man on his left, although all around people seemed to be coming and going.

By the time she had seen her fill, Livy was happy to accept the offer of a coffee. She gave up any vague desire to visit the nearby Peggy Guggenheim Collection, since it was mostly modern art, and instead Livy gave into temptation as she enjoyed a macaroon cake with the welcome drink.

"I think I've had enough art for one day," she said.

"Tomorrow is your last full day here, Olivia. How sad."

"Och, please don't remind me! I love Venice and you've made it even more special, Seb." Livy glanced away at the canal for a moment. "But let's not talk about that since I still have the rest of today, tomorrow, and two evenings to enjoy."

Seb nodded, catching her mood. "You're quite right and we must make the most of the time left to us."

Their conversation eased off a little and Livy suspected they were both thinking of their next parting.

"If you still want to cross the Rialto Bridge, it's not far from here," Seb suggested.

"Absolutely. Can't leave Venice without walking on it."

"I have another suggestion but please tell me to go away if you want to be alone."

Livy laughed, all too aware of how much she was enjoying his company. "Go on, surprise me," she teased.

"You'll have heard of Murano, of glass-making fame? It is very commercial with organised tourist visits, but you might enjoy the boat trip. Burano, the lace-making island is much prettier but would take a little longer so perhaps another time we could go there."

Livy hadn't thought to explore further than Venice itself in so short a time but it sounded interesting. "Do you mean today?" She hadn't missed his suggestion of 'another time' for Burano and hoped that might happen one day in the future.

"Murano is a good place to have a late lunch beside the canal and the fresh fish will have been delivered this morning."

"Yes, okay. I'd never have thought to go there on this trip."

"You might also be glad to get away from the crowds after the Rialto!"

The architecture of the famous bridge was instantly recognisable with the six arches on either side of the centre. They stood in the open part beside the many other tourists enjoying the view down the Grand Canal.

"This was once the financial centre of the western world," Seb said, "but it is now more famous for its fruit and fish markets. This bridge was designed by Antonio da Ponte in 1588, if you wish to know that."

Livy nodded. "I love all the background detail and history." She understood what he'd meant about crowds, as they wandered down the inside steps of the enclosed part that accommodated the many small shops and stalls lining it.

"Well, this wasn't quite what I expected." She laughed at the touristy busyness of it all. By the time she had bought a few small trinkets and a gondola fridge magnet for herself, she was happy to be heading to Murano.

"Should I bring a gift to the party this evening?" she remembered to ask, as they walked down to the canal for the vaporetto, not sure of the etiquette.

"No need, thanks. I'll bring wine from us both."

It didn't take long to board the relevant waterbus to Murano. Livy sat back to admire the scenery, although she was more aware of Seb beside her, their bare forearms touching.

"There seems to be an awful lot of islands," she remarked at one point.

"More than a hundred, I believe," Seb agreed, "although some are uninhabited. One of them has a particularly interesting history, some would say macabre."

They were sitting towards the back of the boat, close together, his arm now casually across her shoulder.

"You *have* to tell me more," Livy said.

"Poveglia is one that few Venetians will mention and fewer tourists will ever hear about, since even the locals are forbidden to visit it these days. Not only was it used for thousands of victims of the Bubonic plague, and then the Black Death, but many centuries later a psychiatric asylum was built to incarcerate the insane, or those thought to be suffering in that way. I don't think many people would wish to visit it, if even some of the stories are true."

"Oh, my goodness, no wonder people stay away. No doubt you're going to tell me it's haunted." She laughed but noticed Seb's expression, then his nod. "It is? You're not kidding me?"

He shrugged. "It might only be a story to keep the young people away, but it does have a terrible reputation."

Livy shivered in the sunshine and Seb pulled her a little closer. "But enough of such tales. This is a day for life and love."

She glanced at his face so close to hers and hesitated at the intensity of his gaze. Before she could move away, he started to lean towards her.

A sudden giggle nearby brought them back to reality. Livy sat back, noticing a couple of young girls watching with interest. Seb grinned at them and pulled her even closer, his arm firmly around her shoulder. But the charged moment had gone.

A multitude of thoughts and emotions rushed through her. Seb's talk of love and the way he held her, confusing her as to *his* thoughts. In two days' time, she would be out of his life again, something she could barely imagine now. Yet what was likely to change? She would soon be back in grey Glasgow, he at his father's vineyards in sunny Tuscany. Perhaps she should avoid seeing him tomorrow, say goodbye after the party tonight? But she was kidding herself.

"Almost here," Seb said, removing his arm to let her gather her belongings. "I imagine you're hungry by now. I know I am! If we wander along by the water, there's a good little restaurant I like to visit when here."

For a moment, Livy wondered who he had brought here before, and the face of the woman she'd seen him with came to mind. Yet he didn't act as though in a relationship. Shrugging the unwelcome thoughts aside, she strolled along content in the more peaceful setting for a short time. The restaurant Seb chose was right beside the canal where they could watch the people wander by. She couldn't wait to try the sea bass and was glad she'd had that cake earlier since they were now into early afternoon. It was worth the wait.

"That was delicious," Livy said as they finished every morsel.

"I thought you'd like it here. We can have a stroll along by the smaller glass-making workshops."

Although the afternoon was at a more leisurely pace than the morning, Livy was aware she wanted to pack as much into these few days with Seb as possible. She had come to Venice alone, expecting to be lonely at times which was why she had booked the cruise, since she would be surrounded by people if she so wished. But everything had changed. How was she supposed to say goodbye to this man again, not knowing if or when their paths might cross in future?

She wondered if similar thoughts might be troubling Seb, or perhaps this was nothing more than a pleasant interlude with an old friend. Yet he had talked of love on the boat over. Maybe everyone talked of love in the same breath as life when in Venice.

They managed to squeeze into one small workshop to watch the famous glass-blowing technique and Livy bought a beautiful green glass-topped bottle opener as a memento and a blue one for Seb, ignoring his protestations.

"I insist," she said. "You have gone out of your way for me."

By the time they returned on the late afternoon boat from Murano, butterflies were fluttering around Livy's tummy in anticipation of the forthcoming party where she would be the only stranger, she assumed. Thankfully she had briefly met Isabella and her husband.

"That was fun, Seb. Thanks for suggesting it," Livy said. "I'd have missed it otherwise."

"It's a while since I've been to Murano, so I was pleased to visit again in your company. Now, I shall leave you to relax before this evening. If it suits you, I'll come to your hotel around seven o'clock?"

"Great. I'll say goodbye here and take my time wandering back. I'd like to browse in a few of the small shops. I think I know my way now."

"Then *ciao,* Olivia, until later." He kissed her cheeks in the manner of any old friend.

She turned and waved once, a little sad that their earlier closeness on the boat hadn't been repeated, yet she was confused enough about her feelings towards him.

Finding what passed for one of the main streets, Livy discovered a few interesting shops, including a stationer which sold unusual cards. Browsing through the selection, she picked out a delicate drawing of the Bridge of Sighs. Inside, she was even more delighted to find a quote from Lord Byron: '*I stood in Venice, on the Bridge of Sighs; a palace and a prison on each hand.*' Perfect.

When Livy went to pay for it, the woman at the counter smiled and engaged her in conversation. "Ah, it was the notorious Lord Byron who gave our famous bridge its romantic name," she said.

"Oh, I hadn't realised that," Livy said.

"He lived and loved here for a while in the eighteenth century and I believe he wrote part of *Don Juan* in Venice, as well as swimming across the lagoon." The woman winked. "I must confess I have always admired the wicked poet."

Livy laughed. "Me too. No wonder Lady Caroline Lamb called him 'Bad, mad and dangerous to know'."

"Of course! I have heard that expression. You are Scottish?" the woman asked.

"I am indeed." Livy was surprised and pleased the accent had been recognised.

"I studied for two years in England and visited relatives in Scotland."

So that explained the faultless English. Livy remembered that many Italians had settled in Scotland, many of them in Glasgow. She said goodbye after a few more pleasantries about Venice, then turned her attention next to the shop that sold Venetian silk scarves and wraps, choosing the one in swirls of lilac and pink for herself. She hesitated at the mask shop, shivering at sight of the grotesque plague masks that reminded her of Seb's story on the boat. No, not today.

Glancing at her watch, she decided instead to return to the hotel for a leisurely bath and pampering before facing the party at Isabella's home. For at the back of her mind was the question she'd been avoiding. Would Seb's mysterious female companion be one of the guests?

Chapter Six

Livy was ready in plenty of time, once again wearing a dress bought for the cruise. She topped it with the Venetian wrap against any sudden chill later on.

Seb was at his most elegant yet casually dressed in the best quality trousers and shirt, a sweater slung across his shoulders.

"You are more beautiful each day, Olivia," he said, after the usual kiss on each cheek.

"You always did know how to flatter a woman, Sebastian." She returned his smile.

"This is not flattery, but fact, *amore*."

Disconcerted by his teasing sincerity, Livy took his proffered hand as they crossed the bridge towards the piazza.

"Is it far?" she asked when they walked straight through the main street, bypassing St Mark's.

"About ten minutes if we take our time. The apartment is further along the canal."

"You don't mean in one of the old palaces?"

"Not quite, sadly, although it's not far from them."

Content to stroll along as they chatted, Livy took deep breaths now and then to quell the nerves fluttering inside. She'd been out with Seb many times years ago in Glasgow, as well as the evenings here, so it must be thought of the party causing the anxiety. Or was it partly because their friendship seemed to be moving on to another level, becoming more serious? Not only was she going to meet some of his friends, but his sister and her husband again. Yet, realistically, how could it make any difference to the fact they'd be parting again too soon?

It was a different kind of bustle in the evening, a far less crowded time to walk through the most popular areas. She was going to miss this but refused to dwell on anything much beyond tonight and tomorrow.

When Seb stopped before a very handsome building, Livy noticed it was almost as old as some of those lining the Grand Canal but had obviously been renovated at some point.

"Here we go," she said in a low voice.

Seb squeezed her hand. "No need to worry, you'll feel right at home very soon and everyone speaks English. Which is good, since I use it mostly myself now, except when I'm at the vineyard."

By the time Livy had been warmly welcomed by Isabella, her husband, and half a dozen guests, her shoulders relaxed. Although some of them chattered in fast Italian to each other now and then, they were all keen to speak to her in a variety of accented English.

"But you are so pretty, Olivia. Where has Sebastian been hiding you?" One of the young women said, turning to her male companion for affirmation.

"Bellisima!" the young man gallantly said, clapping Seb on the back.

Warmth flooded Livy's cheeks at their attention but Seb laughed.

"We keep meeting over the years and so far I've let her get away," he said.

"Maybe it is time to stop, little brother." Isabella had come up in time to hear part of the conversation.

"Perhaps," Seb agreed, winking at his sister. "Or perhaps Olivia only enjoys my company in small measures."

Livy was about to assure him nothing could be further from the truth when another guest arrived. As she watched Isabella greet the elegant woman warmly, Livy recognised her at once. The female she'd seen twice with Seb, in very close conversation both times. She was the type of dark-haired Italian woman that exuded confidence and sex appeal.

Determined not to fade into the background, Livy stood beside Seb as the woman scanned the room, greeted those already there, and made straight for Seb.

"Sebastian! But of course, you are here, *amore*." Wrapping her arms around him, the woman kissed his cheek in lingering fashion before releasing him.

"*Ciao*, Gabrielle." He immediately turned to Livy. "This is my good friend, Gabrielle. Gabby, this is my very good friend from Scotland, Olivia."

Dark eyes surveyed Livy, finely pencilled brows raised in a speculative question mark. Then the red lipsticked mouth curved in a wide smile.

"*Ciao*, Olivia. Sebastian has told me about you." And she kissed Livy on both cheeks as though greeting an old friend.

"Hi. I'm pleased to meet you, Gabrielle." Livy smiled in relief at the woman's friendly welcome, although she couldn't claim any knowledge about *her*. No sign of jealousy in her manner, yet Gabrielle still hooked her arm through Seb's as though to indicate a prior claim.

"You are leaving Venice soon?" Gabrielle asked. "Sebastian said this is your first visit. What a pity it is not longer."

Taken aback at the woman's blunt question, Livy reminded herself that she was indeed nothing but a fleeting visitor into their world. But there was no sound of regret in Gabrielle's words.

"I have one more full day before I leave. Yes, it's my first time here and I hope it won't be the last. It's such a fascinating place."

"Olivia is an art historian with an interest in architecture," Seb explained, before addressing Livy. "Gabrielle also works with art, so you have something in common."

Including you? Livy almost suggested. "I can't believe the wonderful paintings here, even in the churches," she said instead.

Gabrielle nodded, shrugging slim shoulders as though bored. "All the world loves Venice."

Livy was unsure how to respond but Isabella descended on them and steered Gabrielle away to another couple, much to Livy's relief. She'd never felt so gauche or unsure of herself for a long time.

"Don't mind Gabrielle." Seb kept his voice low as he took Livy's arm and moved to the other end of the room. "She's the type of femme fatale that regards every other young female as competition, but she has a kind heart."

Livy smiled at his description but had to ask. "Were you an item? I think I saw you both at Florian's on my first afternoon."

Seb raised his eyebrows. "I didn't realise you'd seen me. You should have mentioned it. No, we've never been quite that close, although Gabrielle has hinted often enough. Not my type, much as I'm fond of her."

So Seb was the one who hadn't succumbed to the siren's call. And no doubt it made the Italian woman even more determined to entice him at every turn. She wondered what type of woman Seb preferred, but it might be better not to ask.

As the evening progressed, Livy watched in appreciation as Isabella provided copious amounts of prosecco and a delicious buffet of cold meats, fish, salads, cheeses and olives, plus tiny delicate panna cotta desserts.

Isabella finally took the chance to speak to Livy, once her guests were happily supplied with food and drink and engaged in their own conversations.

"I am very pleased you could join us, Olivia, as I'm sure Seb is too." She glanced sideways at her brother, a meaningful expression in her eyes.

"Have you been inside the Doge's Palace or the Basilica yet?" Isabella asked.

"No, there seems to be endless queues outside and I didn't want to waste time waiting."

Isabella nodded. "I suspected not. If you are free tomorrow morning, I can get you in before the crowds, if you wish."

"Really? That would be very kind."

Seb interjected. "Sorry, I forgot to tell you that Isabella is a tourist guide at busy times."

"Yes, and I shall give you a private tour," Isabella said. "You need not come, Sebastian, as I want to enjoy Olivia's company to myself."

How could she refuse such an offer? "Then I accept with grateful thanks. I'd given up hope of seeing inside this time." She'd spent so much time with Seb that she'd just enjoyed photographing the outer façade of the buildings. Yet tomorrow was also her last day with him.

As though reading her mind, he encouraged her to see them. "They're quite stunning in parts. Since I'm excluded from the girly chat, why don't I meet you afterwards as there's something else you must experience."

Intrigued, she agreed, pleased to have more time with him but no amount of guessing would make him tell her what he meant.

By the time they were getting ready to leave Isabella's, Livy was in danger of being tipsy. Unused to so much wine, she'd lost track of the number of times her glass had been filled and she'd probably not had enough to eat to soak it up.

They had just said goodbye to their hosts, when Gabrielle sauntered up to Seb and kissed him on the mouth. "*Ciao, amore.*" Her husky Italian voice and musky scent was enough to turn any man's head.

Seb merely held her at arm's length before kissing her on both cheeks. "*Ciao*, Gabrielle. It was good to see you again and to introduce you to Olivia."

Gabrielle smiled with good grace and nodded to Livy before sauntering back to the guests still partying.

When they were finally outside, the cool air hit Livy and she stumbled.

"Better hold on to me, Olivia. I don't think you'd enjoy a dip in the canal."

Seb grinned, seemingly unaffected by anything he'd consumed. Then again, people wouldn't have been plying him with welcome drinks as they had her.

The late evening was a little chillier and Livy was glad of the wrap. She could get used to this strolling along by the Venetian canal with Seb; even the cruise held little appeal after such an unexpectedly romantic interlude. The thought of not seeing him for who knew how long saddened her.

"You are very quiet, *cara mia*." Seb stopped at one of the viewing points by the canal and put his arm around her.

"Mm. I was thinking how much I'll miss Venice after tomorrow." She rested her head against his shoulder.

"Only Venice?" he asked.

She stayed snuggled in to him as she finally replied. "No. This has been so unexpected, meeting you again, spending time with you. But it makes it so much more difficult."

"I know. I feel it too, Olivia, and it scares me."

At that, she pulled away to look at him. "Scares you? What a strange thing to say, from someone who never seems afraid of anything. You've been to so many dangerous parts of the world as a journalist."

Taking her hands, his darkened eyes gazed into hers. "That is nothing compared to matters of the heart. This has reminded me how much I care about you and I don't want to lose you again."

"Me neither." They were silent a moment, regarding each other as though to imprint their image on their minds.

Then Seb leaned forward and touched her lips with his. Rather than pull away, this time he pulled her into a tight embrace as their kiss deepened and Livy's head swam with wine and desire.

"Olivia, *amore*," Seb whispered as they drew breath.

"Don't stop," she said, uncaring if anyone should pass by.

Pulling her close again, he kissed her neck, her face, before claiming her lips again in a deep kiss that reached her soul.

"Your place or mine?" She giggled as they came up for air again. But she sensed at once that she'd spoiled the intimate moment with her silly comment. The wine had loosened her common sense as well inhibitions.

"I do not think that wise, my love, either sneaking up to your hotel room or returning to my sister's, much as I am tempted."

Sobering completely, Livy groaned. "I can't believe I said that. Please forget it, Seb. Och, I'm so embarrassed."

He laughed and pulled her into his side. "I love when you use that expression. It takes me right back to Glasgow and our carefree youth."

She laughed too, thankful he'd lightened the mood, though she still couldn't look at him.

"Listen, Olivia." He waited till she looked up. "I'm as confused as you are about what is happening between us. But you never need to be embarrassed with me. I'd like nothing more than to go to a room and make love to you all night. But I suspect you would regret it more than me in the morning."

Livy nodded, aware that once they crossed that line, their relationship would change forever, with no guarantee it wouldn't be destroyed. "You're right of course. Think the wine went straight to my head, or other parts more difficult to reach."

Laughing again, Seb kissed her cheeks. "Isabella and Luca are always generous with Prosecco and who knows what other combinations. Let's walk so I can see you safely home."

Not entirely over her shame, Livy took Seb's hand, reassured by his quick squeeze. "That was a kind offer from your sister, to show me around the

Palace and Basilica tomorrow. It would be a shame to miss them."

"Don't worry, she loves showing off her knowledge and will want to quiz you, which is why I'm not invited."

"What about?"

"You, me, us mostly." He grinned. "She's always relished her role as my big sister and would like everyone to be as happy as she is."

"There's nothing really to tell, is there?" Livy said, not looking at him.

He was silent so long, she had to glance up. "Seb?"

"Have dinner with me again tomorrow evening, will you?"

Aware he'd ignored her question, she nodded. "I'd like that. Don't want to spend my last evening in Venice alone."

"Remember I'm meeting you after the tour for your first surprise," he said.

"Now I'm even more intrigued." And what did he mean by first surprise? Would there be more?

There was little further conversation as they neared the hotel and once at the door, Seb kissed her briefly before bidding her goodnight.

"I shall see you tomorrow, Olivia. Sleep well."

"Thanks for another great day and evening, Seb." She watched him walk back over the small bridge across the canal, her spirits plummeting at how soon they would be parting, perhaps for ever. No, surely they would meet again. Especially now.

Once in her room, Livy paused by the window when she caught sight of a lone gondola sailing past in the dark canal below. It matched her mood that it was empty of any passengers. She tried to think of only the enjoyable parts of the day and to forget her wanton display this evening. Yet she was also aware that Seb was staying at his sister's apartment where the party might still be going on into the wee small hours. And for all she knew, the beautiful Gabrielle might be waiting to welcome Seb back.

"Stop being such a numpty," she told herself. Seb had already convinced her he had no romantic interest in the woman and hopefully he had also convinced Gabrielle. More than anything, however, Livy had no claim on Seb's heart either, apart from this short flirtation. And she knew fine well what everyone said about holiday romances. How could she have thrown herself at him like that? Yet, she could not mistake his feelings towards her. Much good that might do.

With such depressing thoughts, Livy looked forward instead to being a tourist tomorrow morning with her very own Italian guide to soak up more Venetian history. But most of all, she looked forward to meeting Seb afterwards as it was his face that she longed to see again.

Chapter Seven

After an early breakfast, Livy started rearranging her luggage once she'd sorted out the dresses already worn while here. She'd pack the rest this evening when her departure from Venice was more final. Today, she was going to make the most of the time remaining. It was strange getting ready to go and spend time with Seb's sister, but she liked Isabella and imagined she would learn a lot from her, maybe not only about the buildings.

As she was walking along a couple of quieter streets before the day trippers arrived, she was intrigued to see a work-like kind of barge stopped along one of the canals. She watched for a while, fascinated to see boxes and bags of refuse being hoisted onto the boat by the mini mechanical fork-lift. Seemed everything travelled by water in this city of canals.

Perhaps it was the thought of her imminent departure, but Livy noticed more details as she headed towards St Mark's: the unusual metal sculpture shop sign of a lion rampant above a Trattoria, the water pump with running drinking water in a square and, most intriguingly, an old stone plaque with a lion's head on one wall with what looked like an opening for letters beneath. She'd need to ask Isabella about that.

The nearer she got to St Mark's Square, the busier it became. Livy was pleased she'd gone for a leisurely stroll first to see some of the real Venice and its inhabitants going about their business.

Isabella was waiting outside the Doge's Palace as promised.

"*Ciao*, Olivia. I thought we should start here as this is the busiest place in Venezia."

"I really appreciate this, Isabella," Livy said, after accepting the woman's kiss on the cheek in greeting.

"My pleasure. It gives us a chance to talk, although I shall also tell you about our famous buildings."

Livy smiled, forewarned that the subject of Seb would come up, though she hoped Isabella wouldn't be too disappointed with her meagre answers.

"The Piazza San Marco was seemingly called the Drawing Room of Europe by the great Napoleon and we can see why," Isabella began. "The *Torre dell Orologio*, the clock tower over there, has been telling time for over five hundred years, and below is the lion of St Mark."

Livy had only walked past or through St Mark's until now so was happy to hear more about its features. "What's that?" she asked. "Another clock?" She admired the fancy gold signs and blue centre.

"Ah, that is the zodiacal clock which keeps time in Arabic and Roman numerals. The campanile itself is ninety-nine metres high but offers an excellent view. Now we shall begin your tour."

Recognising several of the astronomical signs, Livy marvelled again at the history of this unique city. It would take many visits to learn all its features and view more than the most famous buildings.

She tried not to feel smug as she accompanied Isabella past the queue already forming outside the palace. She'd have wasted so much time waiting to get into these famous buildings.

Livy had already admired the Gothic entrance to the Doge's Palace but the stairway they ascended was lavish with ornate ceiling carvings.

"This is the *Scala d'Ora*, the Golden Staircase," Isabella explained, and Livy had to agree it was well named.

As she followed Isabella from one room to another, she couldn't quite take in the splendour and opulence everywhere she looked. She stood in amazement in the Grand Council Chamber staring at Tintoretto's painting of *Paradise* which covered one complete end wall.

"This was where they elected the doges and debated state politics," Isabella said. "Then only the nobles were allowed here. Those are the seats of judgement below the painting."

"Wow, that painting alone is worth coming here for," Livy said.

"It is the largest Old Master oil painting in the world." Isabella agreed. "Painted when the artist was seventy years old. There are over three hundred and fifty human figures, I believe."

Livy could believe it. It was mind-boggling how anyone could have painted such a detailed scene, impossible to fully appreciate on a quick viewing but quite stunning to observe in person rather than in a book.

In another room, next to the meeting room of the Council of Ten, Livy noticed a kind of lion's mouth letterbox opening on the wall that reminded her of the one she'd seen outside.

"I noticed a stone plaque with an oblong opening on the way here. Is that for post? Letters?" she asked.

"Ah, you mean the receptacle for secret notes."

"Now that sounds intriguing," Livy said.

"Many times, it was a prelude to intrigue. The council of ten had a secret police-like reputation when discussing matters of state security. Citizens could place their complaints of anything untoward in the letterbox to be delivered here."

"I imagine that must have led to problems at the time." Livy's imagination started picturing different scenarios for intrigue.

Isabella nodded. "Many a person must have been in trouble because of such a secret accusation. The door here leads to the prisons. Visitors are usually only allowed on special tours, but I have permission."

Livy knew she was privileged to get this chance to walk through the long dark corridor that took them to the actual walkway inside the Bridge of Sighs. They stopped part of the way along to peer out from a small gap in one of the windows. Livy was fascinated to see people walking along the footbridge straight ahead at the side of the lagoon, a view of San Giorgio island in the background.

"You are aware that prisoners used to walk across this *Ponte dei Sospiri* after being sentenced? That is why it is named the Bridge of Sighs, as they took their last sight of freedom," Isabella said.

"It's incredible to see the same view as the poor prisoners," Livy replied, aware not many tourists might get this opportunity.

They finally reached the dark prison cells where small barred windows allowed the prisoners a reminder that they were situated above the canal. By the time she'd exhausted most of the palace, relieved to be away from the darker areas, Livy's mind reeled with such history and splendour.

"The Basilica will not take long, then you will be able to meet with my brother," Isabella said as they walked towards the other magnificent building, the queues now even longer.

Livy had wondered when Seb would be mentioned and waited for Isabella's next comment.

"You are an item, as you say?" Isabella asked.

Livy smiled. "Hardly, since we've only just met again after three years."

"And you had not kept in touch?" Isabella's eyebrows rose.

"Not really, apart from an occasional postcard from Seb. Same after university, before we met again at our friend's wedding."

"Yet you seem so close now." Isabella shook her head. "I do not understand. I think Sebastian cares for you very much."

They paused outside the entrance to the Basilica while Livy tried to find the words to explain their relationship, warmth enveloping her at Isabella's assertion.

"We seem to pick up where we last said goodbye, but I'll admit this time seems different. Perhaps because we're older."

Isabella nodded. "Perhaps you have discovered that each other is more important than you realised. But I should not pry. I want you to know that my brother has never truly given his heart to another. There was someone in Tuscany, but it came to nothing."

"Thank you, Isabella. I'm only sad I have so little time here and I don't know where our futures lie."

Isabella nodded but was business-like once more.

"Well let us explore the Basilica, our sumptuous shrine which blends the east and west. The original wooden structure was built in AD 830 as a chapel for the Doges and to house the remains of Saint Mark but it burned down in 976. This magnificent building was completed between 1063 and 1094."

Isabella certainly knew her history, Livy discovered, as she was led around the hushed areas. It had the kind of respectful spiritual air of a church, which she supposed it was, albeit one of stunning beauty. She had worn a shirt over her top, aware that shoulders must be covered in such surroundings.

"Now you must see the great treasure of the *Pala d'Oro* behind the altar."

A treasure indeed, Livy agreed, as she stared at the golden bejewelled altar screen with its many Biblical scenes. "It's absolutely breath-taking." She'd never seen such priceless opulence and was amazed it was on public display like this.

Once she had briefly visited the dark catacombs, she was glad to reach daylight again. Most of the tours had already begun and she could hear subdued voices all around. Outside, the sun blinded her for a moment and all she could see was the lengthening queue of people eager to explore the two buildings. Then she noticed one tall figure apart from the others.

"My brother is eager to see you, Olivia." Isabella smiled, glancing from one to the other.

Livy waved to Seb before turning back to his sister. "I can't thank you enough, Isabella. No photo or picture in a guide book can compare to the real deal."

"It has been my pleasure." Isabella kissed Livy's cheeks then hugged her. "I hope we may see you again very soon and that Sebastian will not lose you again."

Saved from answering by Seb's "*Ciao*", Livy smiled at Isabella as the Italian woman said goodbye before heading back to take some of the waiting tourists on the public tour.

"You survived my sister's enthusiasm then, Olivia?" Seb loosely put his arm around Livy's shoulders.

"Isabella was wonderful and the Palace and Basilica magnificent. I feel honoured to have seen it all with such an expert."

"I'm pleased you enjoyed yourself. Now about that surprise. I imagine you must need a coffee by now, so I've reserved a table for us at Florian's."

They strolled across the piazza. "As you see, it's busy already but I wanted you to have at least one coffee at our famous café."

"What a wonderful idea, but isn't it very expensive?"

"This is my treat, so you must not give it another thought."

"Oh, but I couldn't…" His raised eyebrow stopped her in mid-sentence. "Thank you. I shall accept graciously and gratefully."

"You were kind to a poor lonely student in Glasgow and I've never had the opportunity to repay you."

"As if you were ever lonely." Livy laughed. "You were the most popular guy in our year!" And she was the lucky girl he'd been drawn to from the beginning.

Taking her seat at the small table, placed both to hear the orchestra and to watch the world go by, Livy sighed in pleasure. The music filled their side of the square, the classical notes joyful and light to match the summery air and her mood.

Livy had a look at the menu, eyes widening at the prices. "Do you realise you have to pay more to sit out here with the music?" she asked.

Seb laughed. "Mm, I've been here before, remember? But that's no matter for a special occasion."

Trying to ignore the image of Gabrielle and him together on that first day, Livy focused instead on his words. "Is it a special occasion?"

He took one of her hands, smiling into her eyes. "It is, because we're here together again."

"But then we have to say goodbye tomorrow," Livy kept her voice light to hide her dismay.

"Let's live for today and let tomorrow take care of itself. Meanwhile, here is the waiter approaching," Seb said.

She had already noticed the silver teapots on other tables and wasn't surprised to find the waiter beautifully turned out in a white uniform.

Livy swallowed her reply, deciding he was right. Today was all that mattered for now. After ordering coffee and an almond cake, she excused herself to seek out the facilities, with the ulterior motive of checking out the inside of the café.

Surprisingly, the other tables were in little booth type areas along the front of the building rather than being one large café inside. A very small shop near the entrance enticed her to buy two bars of chocolate, one for her, one for Seb. The cover itself was a souvenir of the famous café. Then she spotted postcards depicting scenes from the past and she bought one to be added to the special little Florian's bag.

The waiter had just arrived when she re-joined Seb. "Sorry, the wee shop waylaid me." She handed him a bar of chocolate once the coffee was served. "A tasty little gift to thank you for all the time you've given me."

"Thank you. You remember my predilection for dark chocolate. But it wasn't necessary as I've enjoyed every minute with you."

They sipped their coffee in companionable silence while Livy absorbed the scene and the music as though it was her last chance.

"How old is this place?" she asked. "I bought a postcard with a scene that looks like the 20s or 30s."

"I believe it's the oldest café in the world, here since the early 1700s. It must have served many a famous person. Did you know that Browning and Henry James and painters like Whistler and Turner spent time in Venice, not to mention Lord Byron, of course?"

She nodded. "Such tales it must have to tell. I've only ever thought of Byron or the infamous Casanova. There was even an episode of Doctor Who set at that time."

"Doctor… Who? Only teasing, I know the programme you mean. Casanova's era was probably the most libertine period of the city, with masked balls and all kinds of intrigue and loose behaviour."

"Don't they still have a carnival?"

"Yes, in February, which is why there are so many masks on sale."

"Oh, that reminds me," Livy said. "I wanted to buy one."

"Then remember to seek out the smaller shops in the alleyways rather than the stalls around here," Seb suggested.

Nodding agreement, Livy watched a young couple saunter past, arms around each other's waist, absorbed in their own private world. Her stomach flipped when she happened to glance at Seb only to find him looking at her.

"The city is full of young lovers at this time of year," he said.

"It must be one of the most romantic places on earth, even more so than Paris, I think," Livy said. "But only if you share it with the right person," she added, her voice catching.

"Olivia…" Seb began, but was suddenly interrupted by a woman's voice.

"*Caio*, Sebastian! How good to see you again so soon." Gabrielle wandered straight up to Seb and waited while he stood up to greet her.

Livy's spirits sank at the interruption. How unfortunately timed, and the woman hadn't even deigned to notice her yet.

"*Ciao*, Gabrielle. I would ask you to join us but, as you see, Olivia and I are having a private conversation."

Bravo, Seb, Livy wanted to say aloud but contented herself with returning the woman's grudging smile when Gabrielle finally acknowledged her.

"But of course. Your leetle friend is leaving tomorrow, is she not?" Again, she addressed her conversation only to Seb. "I am hoping soon to meet my own friends and shall sit over there to watch for them." She gestured to the far end of the café. "*Ciao*." And she wandered away without waiting for Seb's farewell kiss.

For some reason, Livy had the strongest feeling that Gabrielle might be lonely. She surreptitiously glanced over now and then but no one had joined her, although she chatted to any passing waiter while she sipped her coffee.

However, Livy was relieved they were alone again. "You were about to say something?" she reminded him.

"It can keep. I'm very happy to be sitting here with you, Olivia."

She had to be content with that and knew he was every bit aware of Gabrielle as she was. Turning her chair a little towards Seb so she couldn't see the other woman, Livy nodded.

"I'll remind you later, if we're still having dinner."

"Of course we are. I can't let you wander about the lanes of Venice alone on your last evening. Besides, I'll have your second surprise."

No amount of cajoling would make him say another word on the subject and they ended up laughing over reminiscences of their student days.

"Do you have any plans for this afternoon?" Seb asked at last.

"None, apart from taking the vaporetto again for a final sail up the Grand Canal. I'd like to get off at a random stop and wander back through the nooks and crannies, see a little of the city away from the busiest areas." She told him about the refuse collection that morning.

"It's a good idea as most visitors tend to stay around San Marco and thereabouts if time is limited."

Much as she'd enjoyed his company, Livy was looking forward to having another wander by herself and it meant she could explore any church, interesting building or small shops on the way back.

She'd no sooner thought it when Seb took her hand, dropping a light kiss on it. "I look forward to this evening, Olivia. There is something I must attend to this afternoon, but I shall think of you wandering to your heart's content without anyone suggesting what to do."

"I'm looking forward to the evening too, Seb." Even though it would be a bitter sweet final meal together.

By mutual consent, they stood to leave and Livy was surprised when he briefly kissed her lips, rather than the usual peck on the cheeks. For Gabrielle's benefit, perhaps? She'd already noticed the woman still waiting for friends that hadn't arrived.

"Till later, *amore*," Seb said, before heading off in the opposite direction from where Gabrielle sat.

After sitting a few minutes longer, absorbing the atmosphere around the piazza, Livy gathered her bag and sunglasses, about to leave, when Gabrielle stood before her.

"I hope you have enjoyed your visit, Olivia. Sebastian is an amusing escort, is he not? But of course his life is in Italy, at the vineyards in beautiful Tuscany. You will not have seen them?"

Livy guessed exactly what Gabrielle was up to and determined not to play her game. This was nothing more than a brief interlude in Venice and this woman obviously cared about Seb more than he perhaps realised, whether or not he reciprocated.

"Oh, Seb and I go way back to our student days, so I know all about his life." An exaggeration but who cared? "Anyway, I must go, but it's been a pleasure meeting you, Gabrielle. I hope your friends might be along at any moment. Goodbye." She headed across the square before the woman could think of a reply.

Although she tried to ignore Gabrielle's weak attempt to infer a closer relationship with Seb, Livy recognised again how little she really knew about

Seb's life in Italy. Yet she'd never doubted he was telling the truth about his non-relationship with this particular Italian woman. A lot of help that was, however, when she'd be leaving tomorrow.

Chapter Eight

Focusing on her final chance to explore Venice, Livy shrugged off thoughts of the future and concentrated on the magnificent sights ahead of her. Once on the vaporetto, she quickly scanned through her photos of the Doge's Palace and Basilica while they got ready to depart. This time, no elderly couple sat beside her and she turned her back on the other passengers to enjoy the ride along the canal.

She got off at the wooden arched Accademia Bridge and stood in the centre to capture a shot of the canal, laid out like so many paintings of the scene through the centuries. Beautiful. Forced to leave the waterside as there was no path alongside it here, Livy headed up to the inner streets and alleys, crossing small bridges over narrow canals, and soon reached a different square from the previous time.

At one point when she happened to turn the other way, she glimpsed someone who reminded her of Gabrielle, but that was no doubt her imagination embellishing her disquiet about the woman.

She had no idea where she was and couldn't even remember where the marble church lay, but the tables outside a café reminded her she needed lunch. Taking a seat at the furthest away table, she watched the constant passing of tourists even in this less busy area.

Livy stretched her neck and let the patch of sun warm her, completely relaxed and at one with this ancient city, imagining those writers and artists who had enjoyed a similar scene over the centuries.

When she finally got up to leave, she noticed two different routes and purposely chose the narrowest alley. This was what she had imagined, apart from the canals and St Mark's, but she was grateful for the daylight that accompanied her. Venice was relatively safe compared to other European cities, but she'd not care to wander here alone at night. It would be quite different with a friend or lover where every step was an adventure shared.

She fleetingly wondered how different her visit might have been had she not met Seb at the beginning. Yet, wasn't that one of the reasons she'd come alone: to have only herself to worry about for a change, to choose her own destination.

It was a particularly dark alley, the tall buildings on either side leaving little space for daylight and Livy was aware of silence on the paved pathway, apart from her own footsteps. One small balcony caught her attention, adorned by flowers and various windchimes. She took out her camera and aimed it upwards, keen to capture another quirky image to add to a collage, or an online Pinterest board about Venice.

An old-fashioned and dimly lit shop beckoned her in where she found an assortment of tasteful masks. She chose a half-mask in blue and silver, topped by a single feather and tied with blue ribbons. Perfect as a memento and useful should there be a masked ball on the cruise ship.

The sunlight blinded her for a moment when she finally stepped out of the shop, with a friendly *arrivederci* from the owner. She didn't realise anyone was there until she bumped into the woman seemingly hovering outside.

"*Scusi*," Livy said, then glanced up into Gabrielle's eyes. Had she been following her?

"Gabrielle! What are you doing here?" Livy asked at once, before the woman could react.

"Ah, Olivia. How strange to meet you here. My friends had to change our meeting to another day, so I took a leetle ride on the canal instead."

Livy held her gaze, trying to determine the woman's motive. Did she mean to warn her off Seb?

"It certainly is a surprise." Livy didn't know what else to say as she could hardly accuse her of following her.

"Since we have met, why don't we walk along together for a while?" Gabrielle suggested.

Livy shrugged. Why not?

As they strolled through various streets and over the inevitable bridges, Livy was surprised to find Gabrielle an amusing companion, telling her about getting lost in the lanes of Venice, not speaking of Seb at all.

It was Livy who finally mentioned his name. "Have you known Sebastian long?"

"Off and on over the past few years. But he is the only man to resist my charms." Gabrielle smiled at Livy. "You are surprised I tell you this, yes?"

Livy nodded. Everything about this woman was a puzzle. "Why *are* you telling me?"

Gabrielle shrugged elegant shoulders. "I like you, Olivia. You are quite different from his other women."

Livy stopped walking. *Here it comes, a warning off.* She faced Gabrielle but stayed silent.

"I think I know why Sebastian has never settled for anyone. He was waiting for you."

The words were so simple yet sincere that Livy couldn't believe she'd heard correctly.

"I'm sorry. Why are you saying this, Gabrielle?" She still didn't quite trust the woman.

They resumed walking as Gabrielle answered. "It is never going to be me he chooses, and seeing you together today..." She paused before confiding, "I have too much pride to keep hoping for only this one man. Perhaps you will find a way to be together."

Livy's mind was whirling with the woman's words. *Was she for real*?

"I don't know what to say, Gabrielle. Thank you seems inadequate. But there might be little chance of me and Seb being together after I leave."

Gabrielle hesitated again before turning to Livy. "Do not give up yet, Olivia. Love always finds a way, does it not?"

Did it? Livy wasn't sure that was true, and she couldn't imagine how she and Seb could bring their different worlds together. He had commitments in Tuscany, while she had a career she loved in Scotland. She might never find another job so satisfying. True, she no longer had family commitments keeping her there, and her mother would have been the first to tell her to follow her heart. But where exactly was her heart leading her?

"I really appreciate you telling me this, Gabrielle, and I hope we'll meet again."

By this time, they had reached the busy tourist area and Livy held out her hand, making it clear she was saying goodbye.

Ignoring the outstretched hand, Gabrielle kissed Livy on both cheeks. Then she pulled a small business card from her shoulder bag. "If you are ever interested in working in Florence, please call me. We have so many tourists in our galleries that someone like you would be very welcome."

Livy stared at the card. She had assumed Gabrielle lived in Venice. "Oh, you are an art historian too? In Florence?"

"Not so official or professional, but I help at the main galleries. A professional art historian from Britain would be an asset."

Livy shook her head as she stared from the card to Gabrielle. To work in Italy, wasn't that a dream job, now that she had no one dependent on her in Scotland? Yet Gabrielle surely had no real influence over who was recruited in Florence.

"Once again, I don't know what to say. Thank you. It sounds quite overwhelming and I have a lot to think about but it's an exciting idea."

"Then perhaps we shall meet again after all. Why don't you discuss it with Sebastian when you meet this evening? Tell him it is time he too decided on his future." Gabrielle smiled, then called "*Caio*" as she waved and strolled elegantly across the square, hips swaying, until she was out of sight amongst the throng.

Livy still stood staring at the card, impervious to people passing by on either side. Discuss it with Seb? When her future and his seemed always destined to diverge? She pushed the card into her pocket, suspecting it would be ignored until one rainy grey day in Scotland when she remembered this Venetian interlude for what it was: a few days out of normal life with a man she had never forgotten.

Chapter Nine

The whole time she was getting showered and dressed, Livy couldn't stop thinking about Gabrielle's offer. To work in a city like Florence, live in Italy, and more than anything to be in the same country as Seb – what an opportunity.

Then reality kicked in. A casual suggestion was nowhere near the offer of a job. Besides, Seb had his father's vineyard to look after as well as his freelance work. Most of all, however, was the fact that he'd never said he would like their friendship to move on to a more permanent relationship in any way.

No, the card would remain in her luggage to dream over when home, and she had no intention of mentioning it to Seb. She was not going to run after a man who might be best as a friend.

Observing herself in the mirror, Livy reflected that she was taking a long time to choose the right dress and make-up but at least she could leave a lasting impression on Seb, until the next time they happened to meet by chance. Or so she tried to convince herself, all the while acknowledging the ache already taking root in her heart. Perhaps it was the Venetian setting or the romance of the chance encounter, but she couldn't say goodbye so easily this time.

When Seb arrived to meet her, Livy kept her smile firmly in place, any sadness tucked behind a veneer of jollity.

"*Bellisisma*, Olivia. That shade of green suits you perfectly." He kissed her cheek before they headed into the evening streets.

"You're not so bad either." Livy grinned, appreciating the deep blue shirt and fawn chinos; casual yet oh so elegant, enhancing his eyes which smiled into hers and threatened to undo her careful nonchalance about this final evening.

The orchestra still played as they strolled past Caffé Florian, adding to Livy's bitter sweet pleasure.

"I thought you might like to experience one of our local restaurants on the other side of the canal, away from the touristy part," Seb suggested. "The residents know where the best and freshest food is served."

Livy nodded, content to be in his hands this evening, in a manner of speaking, though give her time and she'd be happy to be in his arms before the night was through.

"We'll take the traghetto, the water taxi. It is a tradition to stand on the crossing."

"Oh, I know what you mean. Wasn't that the type of boat used in the film, *Don't Look Now*? You know, the creepy one set in Venice with Donald Sutherland and Julie Christie."

"I've heard of it but never watched it. Something to remedy."

"I won't say too much except that it's well named when you get to the end. Can't believe it began as a short story by Daphne du Maurier."

Seb raised his eyebrows. "It must be some story. So here we are and the traghetto is ready to depart."

It was a short ride across the canal and Livy couldn't help remembering the solemn scene from the film, the women dressed in black as they stood staring ahead. She mentally shook herself. *Stop being so morbid when this evening is full of life*!

Seb took her hand as they stepped from the boat and she kept it in his as they wandered along part of the canal side. They stopped to look across at the campanile and entrance to St Mark's.

"It's strange being on the other side of the usual streets," Livy said.

"I don't think many visitors bother exploring this side, unless they know about the restaurants."

The trattoria Seb took her to was already busy, Italian and Venetian dialects mingling in one big chattering volley of sound. Seb grinned and led her to the table reserved for them.

Livy soon tuned out the other voices as she gave her attention to the menu and the handsome man across from her. Once they'd ordered, Seb took her hand and smiled into her eyes. "Happy with your stay in Venezia, Olivia?"

She held his gaze, determined to be cheerful. "Very. I'll never forget these few days, Seb. It's made Venice so much more special."

"And it's not quite over yet. Remember you have a second surprise," he said.

She'd forgotten his promise of another surprise and, again, he refused to say more. She could only trust it was a pleasant one. The friendly ambience and dimmed lights lulled Livy into forgetting about tomorrow as she talked and laughed with Seb.

At one point, she remembered Gabrielle and her suggestion of Florence, but quickly shelved it again lest she say something before thinking it through.

"Are you looking forward to your cruise?" Seb asked.

"Not as much as I was before arriving here. It wasn't easy going off on my own after Mum died and my so-called relationship broke down. But it seemed like a good idea at the time, and necessary somehow." She still thought so but looked forward to it less than before. "But, you'll be well used to travelling by yourself."

Seb shrugged. "It can get lonely and remind us that life is all about sharing experiences with a special person." He paused before continuing. "But it is also not easy saying goodbye to a surviving parent."

Livy sat up straighter at his words. "I'm so sorry, Seb. I forgot to ask after your father."

"He too passed away, last year."

"And the vineyard?" Livy asked.

Hesitating, Seb finally answered. "One of the reasons I'm here in Venice is to discuss its future with my sister."

"I see." Although she wasn't sure what he meant. "Do you not want to keep it going?"

"That is the question to which I needed the answer."

Livy had a strong suspicion he was only telling her part of the story. Where did that leave him, with his career and location? She was reluctant to probe too deep yet was curious to know where he intended settling, especially with Gabrielle's card on her mind.

"What does Isabella think? If I'm allowed to ask."

"She has always told me to sell it and follow my heart."

How should she respond to that? Before she could, he took both her hands.

"The last time we met, we both had obligations; your mother needed you and my father needed me. But my heart was never in running a vineyard. I want a different future and this time, I hope it includes you."

Now she really was speechless for a moment, while she processed his words and meaning.

"But we belong in separate worlds, Seb." She finally found her voice. "We understood that at Amy's wedding. We can't just change our lives after a few wonderful days together." *Can we?* Should she mention Florence?

"Why not, Olivia? *Carpe diem* and all that. Why not seize the day? I've never stopped thinking about you, though I've tried often enough. So, in the end I did something about it."

She stared at him in confusion. What on earth? "I'm sorry? You've lost me."

"I hope not." He grinned before being completely serious again. "I have a confession to make and I hope you won't be angry."

"Now I'm even more perplexed. Tell me right now, or I'm walking out of here on my own."

She was only half joking, a sinking feeling in the pit of her stomach. Was he going to spoil her last night here?

"No, don't do that, even after I tell you!"

Although he wasn't serious, she noticed his sudden uncertainty. "Go on," she said.

"The day you arrived, and we happened to meet by chance?" Seb said. She nodded. "Well… it wasn't quite such an accident."

Not at all what she'd been expecting him to say. She returned his gaze but kept silent, forcing him to go on.

"Our mutual friend told me you were coming here and since I wanted to visit Isabella, I arranged to arrive at a similar time. I took the chance you'd be happy to see me."

"Amy." It had to be. "You've kept in touch then?"

"Off and on. Evidently, she'd hoped we'd get together at her wedding and was disappointed we went our separate ways again."

Livy shook her head. Amy who had found her own forever love, who commiserated with her when Livy's relationship broke up, who tried to convince her that the right person was out there waiting for her. And had obviously decided his name was Sebastian Leoni.

"I don't know what to say. All this time, I've assumed we met by chance, perhaps were destined to meet again, and you had made it happen." She purposely kept her own voice unemotional, too confused to feel much at all. But she pulled her hands away from his.

"Olivia…" He had to wait while the waiter cleared their main course before continuing. "Dessert?" He asked, but she shook her head. "Coffee?" She nodded.

Once he'd ordered, he tried again. "Please Olivia. I wanted to see you before now, but I believed you were almost settled with someone else and assumed we'd lost our chance."

"For what?"

"Some kind of future together. I'd even be willing to come back to Scotland." He didn't elaborate, and Livy's thoughts were a mess.

"But we didn't really keep in touch after the wedding." That was the kind of friendship they had: pick up where they left off.

"Our priorities lay in separate countries. Until now, perhaps." Seb said.

By the time their coffee was placed in front of them, Livy was in more control. Was this why no one had ever lasted for either of them? It was leading up to this.

"I want to show you something." She retrieved the card from her evening bag and placed it in front of him.

He read it and looked up frowning. "Why has Gabrielle given you her card?"

"We had quite a chat after you'd gone yesterday." She didn't tell him the woman had followed her. "She suggested I might like to work with the galleries in Florence sometime in the future."

Livy enjoyed watching all the emotions playing across his strong face.

"Why on earth would Gabrielle do that?" He shook his head.

"Seems she thinks we deserve each other and thought this might offer a solution to location. Very astute of her."

Seb sat back and regarded her in puzzlement. "And might that be an option?"

Livy shrugged. "I'm still trying to work it out so I wasn't going to tell you yet. But you've given me so much to think about that we might as well add this." She'd kept her face passive while deep inside, she was a mass of excitement, nerves and uncertainties.

Seb laughed aloud at her unemotional words. "Well, you've certainly managed to surprise *me*, as has Gabrielle."

They sat looking at each other, neither speaking and Livy presumed he was deciding what to say next. But he was never at a loss for long, though he glanced at his watch. "We must continue this later. Are you ready for your next surprise?" he asked.

"Absolutely. It's getting a bit noisy here to talk now."

At least the change of scene allowed them to pause the serious conversation, for now. But time was running out and they were hardly any further forward.

Livy assumed they would be taking the traghetto back to the other side, but they strolled along until they could walk across the Rialto Bridge. Seb stopped in the centre so they could gaze out over the darkened canal, the centuries old palazzos a shadowy backdrop, the faint scent of evening blossom from nearby balconies catching the evening breeze.

For one crazy moment, she wondered if he was about to get down on one knee, while her heart raced. But he merely put his arm around her as they watched the few vaporetti and smaller boats negotiate the long canal, one or two mooring at a landing stage to allow passengers access to a hotel.

"It's so beautiful," Livy whispered.

"As are you, Olivia." Seb pulled her into his side in a warm hug.

She had never thought of herself as beautiful, but it made her warm inside to hear him say so in that loving voice. She looked up and after a still moment, their lips met. Then Livy pulled away. How could she bear to leave him tomorrow?

Instead of commenting on her withdrawal, Seb took her hand. "But this is not a surprise. We have to walk only a short distance once we cross the bridge."

Intrigued, and relieved they were back to holding hands, Livy had no idea what to expect. Then, down one narrower canal away from the lagoon, she noticed a single gondola, the young gondolier waiting for someone, his striped top and beribboned straw hat completing the very picture of Venice.

"And here we are, *cara mia*," Seb said.

Livy stared in delight. They were so expensive that she'd given up any idea of a ride in a gondola, especially on her own. But this was the perfect end to her short break.

"*Bueno noche*," Seb said to the gondolier, confirming his own name.

"*Bueno noche, signor, signorina*. The night is beautiful, is it not?"

Livy nodded agreement and remembered to thank him as she continued to stare at the long curved black boat with the red covered seats.

"Please to sit," the young man said.

Seb took Livy's hand as she stepped in, following behind her. "The seat in the centre is ours and the gondolier will stand at the back," Seb said.

Livy carefully sat down on the low seat, smiling as Seb folded his longer frame beside her. They faced the front, away from the gondolier who held their adventure in his hands, while Livy tried to quell her excitement. It reminded her vaguely of the punts in Cambridge, the boat propelled only by aid of a long pole in expert hands. But this was one of the most romantic cities in the world and she was sitting on a gondola with the man she... yes, she loved.

Relaxing back against Seb's arm, Livy breathed a sigh of pleasure. Whatever else happened in the next week, or month, or year, she would long remember this interlude and especially this evening.

"Thank you," she whispered to Seb.

He squeezed her shoulder. "It is my pleasure, Olivia. I wanted your last evening to be special."

As they made their way through the narrow canal, Livy watched the ancient buildings pass by, some festooned with colourful window boxes to relieve the grey stone or enhance the salmon pink brick, others adorned with small balconies that made her think of Romeo and Juliet. It gave her a different perspective, gliding along in the age-old gondola as many had done in the past. No matter that these were mostly for tourists, it made her feel part of the tradition.

Just when she'd decided it couldn't get much more romantic than this, the tenor voice of the young gondolier echoed in the night air as he began to sing.

"Oh my goodness. Did you arrange this?" Livy asked, remembering reading that this was extra.

"He sings better than me," Seb quipped.

Livy smiled and snuggled closer as they reclined like royalty while the gondolier serenaded them with a couple of Italian songs, all the while manoeuvring them down along another canal and under a low bridge. The notes of the final song ended when she realised they were gliding along part of the Grand Canal into St Mark's basin.

"Oh, we're about to pass under the Bridge of Sighs," Livy said.

"Enjoying your second surprise, Olivia?" Seb whispered in her ear.

"Mm. This is the life and to think I might have missed this experience." She tilted her face to his. "Thank you, dearest Seb."

For answer, he closed the tiny gap between them and met her lips in a lingering kiss. As they parted, she thought she heard a church bell. Imagination?

Seb kept his arm close around her. "There is a legend that says if a couple in a gondola kiss as they pass under the bridge at sunset, while the bells of St. Mark's toll, their love will last forever."

If that love ever had the chance, Livy's practical self silently whispered. *Yet, hadn't she just heard a bell*? Her heart argued.

"How romantic," she answered at last, as they were passing the landing stage of her hotel before carrying on under the small bridge to take them back to where they'd started.

It reminded Livy of her arrival by motorboat and the difference a few days had made to her life. And possibly to her future? But where did they go from here, when all too soon she would be saying goodbye.

When they finally stepped from the gondola, with many an *arrivederci*, Livy took a moment to regain her land legs.

"Oops-a-daisy," she said, laughing as Seb caught her to him on the small bridge near her hotel. "And it's definitely not because of alcohol," she assured him.

They stood locked together on the bridge, alone for once in this usually busy crossing place.

Seb pushed a strand of hair from her eyes. "I think I love you, Olivia."

She caught her breath before replying. "You think?" she teased. "Well, I think I love you too, Sebastian, not only as a friend."

As though to seal their declaration, their kiss this time deepened and Livy sagged against him when it finally ended.

Trying to catch a tear before it threatened to fall, she buried her head against his chest, welcoming his arms around her.

"What happens now?" she managed at last.

"Let's see what the next week or so brings when we leave here."

She looked up at him. "You're leaving too?"

He nodded. "It wouldn't be the same without you and I've more or less decided to sell the vineyard, with Isabella's agreement."

By mutual consent, they continued their stroll over the bridge and along the narrow streets towards her hotel.

"Are you being escorted to the ship tomorrow?" Seb asked.

"The tour company has arranged for someone to pick up my case but I'm getting the vaporetto to the ship terminal. I don't think it's far since it's not one of those mega ships."

They skirted around the imminent parting from each other until they reached the hotel.

"Will you keep in touch with me this time, Seb?"

"Of course. I meant it when I said I don't want to lose you, Olivia."

"Then I suppose this must be goodbye." While her words seemed calm, inside she was crying. He hadn't even offered to see her off.

"No, only *arrivederci, mi amore*." Seb bent his head and claimed her mouth once more in a lingering kiss. "*Ti amero per sempre*," he whispered in her ear. "I'll always love you."

She had to stop herself from inviting him up to her room, to spend one passionate night together. But she couldn't do it, as it would only remind her of what she was missing. Better not to have tasted what she couldn't have.

When they drew apart, Seb touched her face but only said, "*Ciao*, Olivia. We shall meet again very soon." And he turned away before she could call him back.

Chapter Ten

Throwing the remainder of her clothes into the case, Livy took her last evening view of the canal, pausing when she noticed a gondola gliding past, carrying a happy couple enjoying their moment of romance.

Sighing, she eventually fell into bed and tried to read for a while, but tears blurred the words and she gave up. She tossed and turned all night, remembering every moment she and Seb were together. So much for looking forward to a lovely cruise tomorrow.

Tired after her unsettled night, Livy ate a quick breakfast to keep her going and was ready to greet the representative from the tour company who took her case. The middle-aged Italian was cheerful but not talkative which suited her fine. Making sure she knew the correct stop to get off the vaporetto, he waved goodbye with the usual "*Ciao, signorina*" as Livy thanked him. At least the case would be taken to the cruise terminal for her.

As the water bus sailed away from St Mark's in the opposite direction from her trips on the Grand Canal, Livy sat and watched the Campanile and Doge's Palace fade from view. The new adventure was about to begin, and she had decided to embrace it. Who knew what might happen once she was back home? She and Seb both had decisions to make about their future and she could only hope they might find a way to make it together. She was a little disappointed that he hadn't come to see her off but perhaps he, too, didn't want to prolong their farewell.

A few other passengers looked as if they were also going to the ship, mostly couples who had probably spent a day or two in Venice first. When they arrived at the cruise terminal, Livy was pleased to find all the cases being taken care of by smiling men in work uniforms who indicated she would eventually find hers in her room on board the ship. She joined the short queue forming inside the departure building, finally feeling a little frisson of excitement at exploring new places, even if it had to be alone. Thankfully, she'd got here early as more people kept arriving.

It would take her a long time to forget these past few days, but better to be going somewhere new rather than home to boredom and grey skies, and lonely thoughts of what might have been.

When she reached one of the check-in desks, the young woman greeted her warmly. After taking her passport to be returned later, she took Livy's photo with a tiny camera on a stand.

"Welcome to your cruise. I'm sure you'll have a wonderful journey with us," she said, all smiles, her accent American or Canadian.

Livy returned the smile and thanked her, hoping she was right. She was then pointed in the direction of steps by another smart member of staff. Following several other people, she soon found herself ascending the gangway and entering the actual ship at last, to be greeted by two white uniformed personnel.

"Welcome aboard," a young man said. "Please make your way to the dining room and enjoy a buffet lunch until your stateroom is ready."

Livy couldn't stop smiling at everyone's air of bonhomie and genuine welcome. Stateroom sounded so grand, but she knew it was the usual name for what people used to call their cabin. No doubt since most ships were now rather more luxurious than a boat with cabins.

She took her time wandering along a couple of the decks before finding the correct one for lunch. At every turn, a pleasant member of staff directed the new arrivals and Livy smiled in return. The only regret so far was the fact she was alone, although surely there would be other singles like her.

Single. It sounded so lonely after being part of a couple for the last few days and she wondered what Seb was doing this morning, whether he too was leaving right away, albeit by plane perhaps.

Livy climbed another flight of stairs, the sudden buzz of voices telling her she must be near the dining room. Then just before she reached the open doors, she stopped dead. Standing nonchalantly against the wall along from the dining room reading a leaflet, was Sebastian, as large as life.

Livy blinked and stared. Perhaps she had conjured him up by thinking about him. Or was it only another guy who looked like him? The man looked up as though waiting for her and winked.

Hurrying over, out of the way of other passengers, she stopped in front of him.

"I don't believe it! What are you doing here, Seb? Have you come to see me off? I didn't think non-passengers were allowed on board."

"Slow down, Olivia." Seb laughed. No, I'm not here to say goodbye. I too am a passenger."

Speechless for a moment, Livy shook her head." You mean you're booked on this cruise? How is that possible?"

Then she remembered he'd already known when she would arrive in Venice so maybe he also knew when she was leaving and on which ship. "Not Amy again?"

He came up beside her and led her to a more private area away from the busy dining room entrance.

"No. I couldn't take it for granted you'd welcome my company that long. But the past few days have been more than I could imagine, and I managed to get one of the very last vacant rooms yesterday. I didn't care if it was their worst or best, if it allowed me to travel with you. This is your final surprise, my darling Olivia."

Livy shook her head, trying to take in his words, still doubting the evidence, unable to believe this was not goodbye. Her heart was skipping a beat at thought of the days and nights ahead, pleased he'd taken nothing for granted.

Throwing her arms around him, Livy gazed into his precious face. "This is the best surprise of all."

She was glad of their little bit of privacy as they clung together, their kiss deep and promising.

As they eventually headed into lunch, Livy smiled in complete contentment. A new adventure was about to start with Seb, one which would soon enter uncharted waters, as a couple. Her heart warmed at the thought. He had proved his commitment to her by being here. From this moment on, they would face the future together, wherever it might take them. This was only the beginning of an exciting journey.

Published Books

The Highland Lass
Return to Kilcraig
Dangerous Deceit
Mischief at Mulberry Manor
Midwinter Masquerade
Pride & Progress
The Aphrodite Touch (1st in series)
The Adonis Touch (2nd in series)
The Aphrodite Assignment (3rd in series)

Beneath the Treetops (short stories)
End of the Road (short stories)
Two of a Kind (short stories)
Romantic Encounters (short stories)

Summer of the Eagles
The Jigsaw Puzzle

Rosemary Gemmell lives in beautiful Scotland and is a prize-winning freelance writer of short stories, articles and poetry, many published in UK magazines, online and abroad. She is the author of historical and contemporary novels and tween books.

Rosemary is a member of the Society of Authors, the Romantic Novelists' Association and the Scottish Association of Writers.

You can subscribe to her newsletter on the website or blog for up to date news and occasional special offers and competitions.

Printed in Great Britain
by Amazon